"Let them catch up to us," Bolan ordered

"When I yell 'step on it,' I mean right away and move like a bat out of hell," he added.

As he expected, the limo drew up to their right side. The Executioner didn't wait for the guns. He jerked the M–67 grenades free, pulled their pins, counted to four and lobbed the bombs into the vehicle.

"Step on it," Bolan shouted. "Pull in to that side street and stop the car."

As he and Tolstoy got out of the vehicle they saw the fierce burst of flame lighting the area behind them. The shock waves from the explosion shattered nearby windows, and a shower of metal and glass rained over them.

"Time to get out of here," Bolan said as he got back into the GAZ.

He hoped the message to Donielev would be clear: time was running out for him and his kind.

MACK BOLAN ®

The Executioner

DON PENDLETON'S
EXECUTIONER®
THE
FISSION FURY

A GOLD EAGLE BOOK FROM
WORLDWIDE®

TORONTO • NEW YORK • LONDON
AMSTERDAM • PARIS • SYDNEY • HAMBURG
STOCKHOLM • ATHENS • TOKYO • MILAN
MADRID • WARSAW • BUDAPEST • AUCKLAND

First edition October 1996
ISBN 0-373-64214-8

Special thanks and acknowledgment to
David North for his contribution to this work.

FISSION FURY

Printed in U.S.A.

Danger—if you meet it promptly and without flinching you will reduce the danger by half. Never run away from anything. Never!

—Winston Churchill
1874–1965

Those who have spent their lives trying to destroy won't stop just because they claim they're different. They'll only find new ways.

—Mack Bolan

In memory of David North

PROLOGUE

Oleg Aliyev parked his rusting Moskvitch on the deserted side street and waited. The Proletarsky district was empty at this late hour. None of the factories—not even the huge Likhachev truck-manufacturing plant—stayed open for a third shift.

He knew a lot about manufacturing trucks. He had worked at Likhachev until they had laid him off for some minor infraction of the rules. The department manager had made such a big deal about catching him taking a handful of gears. As if he were the only one in the factory doing it.

Lucky for him, he had convinced his aunt that he wanted to start a new career, something with a future. She had gotten him a position as a technician at the Obrinsk Research Institute. It was a good job, full of potential. But it didn't pay enough—not to cover the money he owed to the small gambling casino located in the basement of the building next door to his apartment building.

The money he had received from selling the nuclear fuel rods he was able to smuggle out of the institute didn't quite cover his debts.

But Lady Fate had been good to him. Just when he was facing exposure for the thefts, and prison, she had given him an opportunity to make enough money to pay what he owed and even quit his job if he wanted.

Dr. Polsky, one of the senior researchers at the institute, had taken him aside.

"Oleg, I know what you've been doing," the elderly scientist had said.

Certain the man was planning to turn him in, the young technician begged for mercy. Instead of responding to his plea, the senior scientist asked him a question.

"To whom do you sell this material you steal?"

Aliyev remembered how nervous he was.

"There are always people who will buy such things."

"The Russian mafia?"

The young technician didn't know if the man who'd been purchasing the fuel rods was in the mafia, but it seemed safe to assume so.

"It is my understanding that the mafia can be helpful in arranging all sorts of things," Polsky continued. "Such as helping people arrange their own kidnapping. For a fee, of course."

Aliyev began to understand what the elderly researcher was asking. Could he introduce Dr. Polsky to someone in the mafia who could set up a fake kidnapping?

"I would also have to get a fee," the young man warned.

"Let me discuss it with my two associates. If we wish to go any further, I assume you can arrange a meeting."

Aliyev thought of the attractive brunette who was his aunt's assistant, with whom he'd been having an affair—Lieutenant Lena Kurilov, aide to Colonel Irina Tolstoy, deputy chief of security for the Ministry of Atomic Energy.

In the past his aunt had questioned him about the disappearance of supplies. That morning she'd interrogated him about the missing scientists, and he had admitted that he had driven them to meet someone who might be able to help them with their request.

Technically he knew he was under arrest. But that meant something only if he stayed in Russia. And he intended to leave the country as soon as he collected his money.

The car he had been waiting for arrived. There were two men sitting in it, and he knew one of them: Vasily Federov.

From the way the man carried himself, Aliyev was sure he had been in the military before he joined the mafia. He had heard others call Federov "Colonel."

In fact Federov had been a colonel, but in the KGB.

"Get inside," the former colonel called out.

The young technician left his car and climbed in the back of the Volvo. The seats were covered in leather, and he wished Federov had removed the plastic seat covers so he could smell the rich aroma of cured animal skins.

He smiled at the men in front. "The three scientists arrived safely?"

"Right on schedule," Federov replied.

"I am certain you can help them," Aliyev continued.

"The general has no doubt about that."

Aliyev didn't know the name of the man for whom Federov worked. All he knew was that he had been a general once.

"So all that remains is for me to collect my fee and vanish."

"Exactly," Federov agreed.

The young man could already feel the warm sun of the Caribbean.

He leaned forward as Federov turned to face him. Instead of an envelope filled with hard currency, the former colonel held a Tokarev pistol in his hand.

Aliyev started to protest, but before he could speak, two rounds drilled into his open mouth and exploded into his brain.

Federov nodded to the driver, who got out and opened the rear door. Tugging at the still form, he let it roll into the rough asphalt street, then got back in the car and drove away.

1

Aleksandr Polsky was going to have to die.

Yuri Donielev had made the decision in the past five minutes.

For the past twenty-four hours, the former KGB major-general had listened to his whining and intellectual posturing. He was getting tired of it.

Donielev was a busy man. It wasn't easy running one of the largest mafia gangs in Moscow, especially when the people who led the other gangs kept protesting his invasion of what they considered their exclusive businesses.

Their protests often took the form of pitched gun battles, sometimes in midday on crowded central-Moscow streets. Several times in the past month, the cars his men used had been wired with bombs designed to detonate at the turn of an ignition key or when the car started to move.

Keeping a step ahead of the other godfathers was a full-time job. There was no council of mafia leaders similar to the one he had read existed in the United States, where the various bosses could bring their complaints and get decisions that were binding on all the gangs.

Not that that would have stopped him. But at least he could find his rivals all together in one room. And eliminate them.

Now this short, elderly man from the Obrinsk Research Institute thought he had the right to impose on his time with foolish discussions about virtue, honor and loyalty.

Donielev had brought Dr. Polsky and his two top assistants to his luxuriously furnished dacha outside Moscow to discuss helping them stage their own kidnapping. Now the bearded scientist had changed his mind and wanted to go back to the institute.

The ex-KGB officer was frustrated. Didn't anyone live up to his agreements any more?

He would try one more time to reason with the old man. "Reconsider your decision," he said in a deceptively soft voice. "Are you not comfortable here?"

Seated in front of a roaring fire in the large stone living-room fireplace, the elderly man with a graying goatee turned and stared at his host.

"You have been a good host," Polsky said. "You've shared your beautiful home with us. Our bedrooms upstairs are each larger than an apartment that accommodates a family of four."

He looked around at the art treasures mounted on the walls: ancient tapestries, rare icons from Russian monasteries, paintings that had, until recently, hung in museums.

"You have treasures that I have never seen outside of a museum," Polsky commented. "But I will return to the institute in Obrinsk with this." He put both of his hands around the large lead cylinder that contained a kilo of the improved, weapons-grade plutonium 239 he and his assistants had been developing.

He turned to the other two seated men. "If you were wise, you would come with me and confess, too."

Associate Professor Leonid Sartov shook his head. "They will arrest you. Perhaps they will send you to Lefortovo Prison to be tortured."

"That is a risk I must take," the old man said. "But for my own conscience I must go back."

The third scientist, Boris Davidov, a short, thin man with almost no color in his face, shook his head. "Go back to what? We are paid less than a bus driver in Moscow. Finally we have a chance to leave this cursed land with enough money to live comfortably." He looked at the two well-dressed men sitting across the small room and winked. "Even after we share with our new friends the reward for finding us."

Sartov glared at the dissenting scientist. "We will go back, Aleksandr. But only after the reward money for our return is paid. The government will get back its plutonium, and after a few months, we can announce our decision to migrate to someplace else. Like the United States or, perhaps, someplace glamorous like Switzerland or the South of France."

Polsky became cynical. "What makes you think the government will let us leave? What we have been working on is so top secret that not even many government officials know about it."

The other scientists knew their colleague was right. The three had been kept in a separate laboratory to develop new technology that would make the transporting of plutonium less dangerous without reducing its weapons potency. They had found a way to reduce the alpha-rays emissions substantially, which meant the nuclear material could be carried in substantially smaller and lighter containers.

"Any country with knowledge of how to do this can manufacture nuclear bombs and ship them anywhere with only the smallest risk of having them detected. This means that our bitterest enemies can make such bombs and plant them in such places as the Kremlin without our being the wiser," Polsky warned.

"The more reason to collect our money and get out," Sartov replied. "Russia has many enemies."

"So do the three of us," Polsky replied. "Anyone who wants to manufacture such a bomb is our enemy. Or rather, we are their prey."

Donielev stood with his back against a brocaded wall and listened. He was dark skinned like his ancestors, who came from the Caucasus. Even at sixty, he had maintained the body of a wrestler by working out daily in his private gym. His short, wide body was covered in a custom-tailored suit. He had shaved the thinning hair from his head, which gave him a somewhat sinister appearance.

The former KGB division head had been responsible for the deaths of thousands—many of them innocent men and women—before the organization had been dismantled. As head of the Second Directorate, Donielev had the freedom to investigate and eradicate anyone he chose—dissidents, officials, even others in the KGB itself.

Until he was deposed, his name had made even the powerful in the Soviet Union quiver with fear. Like the KGB itself, the Second Directorate he ran was a terrifying, repressive monolith that controlled the lives of ordinary Soviet citizens and most of the country's leaders.

Now just a businessman, as he described himself to outsiders, Donielev controlled a great variety of criminal activities through the large mafia gang he ran: prostitution, drugs, protection, blackmail, kidnapping, contraband merchandise, the sale of stolen weapons and military equipment, even nuclear fuel. Nothing happened in Moscow without him getting his percentage.

The huge profits from his various enterprises had bought him the pair of Mercedes-Benz vehicles parked outside. The dacha and the various properties he owned—farms, warehouses, factories—the clothes he wore, custom-tailored by an Englishman who flew to Moscow just to fit him, even the special French-made cigarettes he smoked were paid for with a fraction of the monies his men had collected.

He turned to the young woman who stood next to him. "The old man is causing me more aggravation than he is worth," he whispered.

The young dark-haired woman who stood at his side was expressionless. The expensive, dark-colored wool suit she wore—a gift from Donielev—accentuated her slim figure.

Lena Kurilov's face wasn't pretty, but with the aid of the French-made cosmetics the former general had given her, the thirty-year-old woman gave the appearance of being attractive.

"When Oleg Aliyev came to me with their proposal to help them fake their own kidnapping for a third of the ransom, it sounded like such an easy way for both of us to make money," she whispered, apologizing. "I suppose you will have to let Polsky go back."

"Too dangerous. For *all* of us."

"Even with Aliyev dead?"

It was only prudent, Donielev had decided, to have the young technician killed. The fewer who knew about his involvement in the affair, the safer it was for him.

Donielev looked at his three visitors. "They know," he reminded her.

Kurilov shrugged, then looked at her wristwatch. "I will be in trouble if I am not back in my office within the hour. Colonel Tolstoy still distrusts everyone like she did when we were both with the KGB," she whispered. "I have to get back into my uniform. I will call you in the morning. Let me know what you decide to do."

He nodded. It didn't matter to him whether the woman stayed or left. She was a pleasant temporary diversion. The three men seated in the room represented a huge sum of money. They were an unexpected gift brought to him because of his expertise in such things as kidnapping.

The kidnapping of the nuclear specialists hadn't been his idea. The three scientists had conceived the plan themselves as a way of getting enough money to leave Russia and settle someplace else.

Their plan had been simple: pretend to be kidnapped, along with a small quantity of the new plutonium 239 fuel. Once the ransom was paid, they and the nuclear fuel would be returned.

After a year or so, they would announce their intention to emigrate to another country, where their two-thirds share of the money would be waiting.

Donielev found only one thing wrong with their plan—his share of the ransom. He wanted it all. And more.

He knew an American named Maxwell Haverford—like himself, a former Intelligence official. Retired from the CIA, Haverford now acted as a consultant to companies and governments, including his own CIA.

And, of course, Yuri Donielev.

The American had agreed to market the nuclear scientists and their new plutonium to one of his own clients, for as much as he felt he could get from them. Half of the money would be his fee.

The most likely buyer, the American felt, were the Iranians.

Donielev was waiting for the American to call to say the deal was set. Then, once Haverford had collected the money, he could put the two scientists on a plane bound for Tehran and enjoy the financial rewards for a job well-done.

The ex-KGB officer walked to a nearby wall and pushed a small buzzer.

Within seconds a well-dressed, dark-haired man with black bushy eyebrows entered the living room.

"One of our guests will need transportation tomorrow morning, Vasily," he said with a hard smile. "You can use the beige Volvo—the 760."

Federov had worked for the general for many years, as a full colonel and Donielev's personal aide in the KGB. When the general had told him to use the Volvo, he knew what his superior meant: kill the man and dispose of his body.

EVEN IN THE BRIGHT fall daylight, Donielev's dacha on the western outskirts of Moscow was a showplace. Sitting on a secluded plot along Rublyovskoy Shosse, forty miles from the center of the Russian capital, the two-story brick structure was guarded by a high stone wall that surrounded the property.

This greenbelt that circled Moscow was where the politically powerful leaders of the Soviet Union had once spent their weekends. And where the powerful and influential of the Russian Federation now got away from the pressures of work.

The difference was that only those with political or military power had lived in dachas before the disintegration of the Communist confederation. Now those who had the hard currency could acquire one.

Federov left the living room and went outside to get the car ready.

Six of his best men—hard-faced veterans of the street—leaned against the outside walls of the house, constantly scanning for signs of unwanted observers. Each cradled an AK-74 assault rifle fitted with a 30-round clip in his arms.

One of the guards shivered and buttoned his woolen jacket. "Damn," Kasim Mutalidov griped, "it's only September and already it's getting cold. It's probably twice as warm back home."

Emerging from the house, former KGB Colonel Vasily Federov stared at the complainer. "Stop griping, Kasim," he snapped. "Back in the village of Stepanakart, you were only a poor enforcer for a local gang. Here in Moscow you are a wealthy member of a powerful family, with all the privileges that go with it."

The hardman looked sheepish.

"It does get cold early in Moscow, Colonel. There's frost already. You should have warned me when you asked me to join up. I would have brought warmer clothes."

"How long have you been with us?"

"Five months."

"You learn slowly, my friend. We don't buy things. We go to the stores we offer protection to and take what we want."

He turned to the other guards. "The general has a job for you in the morning. Have the large Volvo ready," he ordered.

The hard men looked at one another with silent understanding.

Using the Volvo, with its plastic seat covers, meant that somebody was going to die.

"MOSCOW HAS CHANGED more than you can imagine since you were here last," the stout driver told Mack Bolan.

"It hasn't been that long ago. In what ways?"

"Every way. Look around you," Andrei Gorsky said. "Does anything look the same as it did when you were last here?"

"I didn't have the luxury of doing much sight-seeing then. But life here does look a little more frantic."

"Then take my word. Things keep getting different."

As Gorksy drove his ancient vehicle through the center of the city, Bolan was surprised at how much Gorsky had changed. The last time they had seen each other, the man was well-groomed and wore well-cut business suits. Now his hair was long and unkempt. A worn peaked cap kept it from flying into his eyes. The leather jacket that covered his body was lined with the creases of age.

"You're different, too, Andrei," the Executioner commented. "Marriage must be working."

"I have a family now that needs supporting. So I do anything I can to put food on the table and a roof over their heads." He caught himself. "Almost anything. I try to be a good example for my two little children."

The man behind the wheel had met Bolan outside the airport in response to the international call the soldier had placed. Andrei Gorsky had been a bodyguard to a mafia leader who had turned against his silent partners—ex-KGB department heads—to assist Bolan, and was murdered by them. Thanks to the American's help, Gorsky had escaped his employer's fate.

"I owe you, my friend," he had told Bolan when they'd parted company. "I always pay my debts."

Gorsky had become a jack-of-all-trades, surviving by doing favors. What Bolan liked about the man was that he didn't pretend to be honest. But he never betrayed a friend or his current employer.

As they stopped for a red light, the stocky man asked, "What hotel are you staying at?"

"The Zolotoye Kolsto."

Gorsky shrugged. "It's clean and efficient." He swerved around pedestrians crossing the street. "It's a long drive from here. We will have time to talk."

The last time Bolan had been there, Moscow was a city in turmoil. People were still bewildered by their new freedom, by the absence of the hated KGB. Everyone in the city still stared at one another with fear, wondering who, if any, were informers. Few had yet digested the fact that they were living in a country that no longer had secret police peering around every corner.

As they drove through central Moscow, people on the street seemed to move at an even more confident pace, ignoring the occasional presence of a uniformed police officer.

The young people wore jeans and leather jackets like their equivalents in the United States. The sound of rock-and-roll music pouring from boom boxes shattered the air.

Everywhere he looked, Bolan saw evidence of Muscovites trying to mimic Americans.

There were long lines of people waiting to get into McDonald's, and foreign cars lined the streets of central Moscow.

"Different, isn't it?"

Bolan was too busy studying the people to reply.

"Let me show you something," Gorsky said, and turned a corner.

Pedestals that formerly supported Soviet heroes stood empty in city plazas, waiting for new heroes to take their place or for the old ones to be absolved and reinstated. Numerous churches had been destroyed or turned into warehouses or offices in the Soviet era. Those that could were now being rebuilt or refurbished with a love that Muscovites had feared to exhibit under the Soviet regime.

Neon advertisements selling everything from cigarettes to vodka to hamburgers were shining from the rooftops of Stalinist-era buildings. Gleaming new hotels built by Western companies were a startling contrast to the dilapidated buildings hidden behind shaky scaffolding next door to them.

"We have become so American we have gambling casinos and nightclubs and pornographic shows all over the city. And prostitutes on every corner and in the lobby of every hotel," the driver commented with a hint of disgust in his voice.

While most of the nine million inhabitants had neither the desire nor the money to participate in the various entertainment establishments that had sprung up throughout the city, thousands of nouveau riche Russians, mafia members, black marketers and Western visitors could and did.

Mack Bolan had studied the Intel reports Hal Brognola had provided on the flight to Moscow. From the reports he had read, he knew that housing was still in extremely short supply. To obtain an apartment in a relatively decent neighborhood could command a bribe of a hundred thousand dollars or more in hard currency. Most Moscow residents still crowded whole families into one-room apartments—or, if they were lucky, into one bedroom units.

Russians still had to wait in line to try to purchase daily necessities. But the old state shops had been mostly replaced by endless rows of makeshift wood kiosks offering a bewildering array of foods and goods. Some sections of the city had become twenty-four-hour flea markets, making it possible for residents to shop at any hour.

As they continued driving, Bolan noted that the wealthy still had their own shops, as they had under Soviet rule. Tverskaya Street, in the city's center, had become the Fifth Avenue of Moscow. Exclusive shops offering imported fashions, cosmetics, jewelry, even cars, lined the street.

Gorsky turned into New Arbat Street. The stores that faced it displayed a wide variety of imported goods. Antique shops filled the street, run by dealers who claimed to have available rare icons, once the property of different Russian Orthodox monasteries. Many were clever forgeries aimed at art-hungry foreign collectors willing to buy stolen relics.

Stopping for a red light, Gorsky glanced at the large man who sat next to him.

"I can see in your face that much has happened to you since last we saw each other. Why are you here?"

There was only so much Bolan felt he could share. "I'm looking for three men. Scientists. They've disappeared."

"Voluntarily?"

"I'm not sure if they took off or if someone took them."

Gorsky shook his head. "Kidnapping has become the latest industry in Russia. Every petty thief is kidnapping somebody and holding them for ransom. How important are the three missing scientists?"

"Very important. Not only to Russia, but to the whole world."

The Russian became quiet. Finally he made a suggestion. "I know a man who seems to have all kinds of information about criminal activities in Moscow. A kind of a broker. He sells information."

"How much?"

Gorsky thought for a minute. "Can you afford five hundred dollars?"

Bolan reached in his pocket and started to take out the money.

"No. Give it directly to him after he tells you what you want to know."

"When can we meet him?"

"Right now, if you want. He hangs out in Ismailovsky Park."

The Executioner nodded. "Now is as good a time as any. The sooner I find out where they are, the sooner I can finish my business here."

Gorsky remembered how the American had finished his "business" the last time—by destroying the ex-KGB officials who were shooting their way into the mafia.

He was glad he wasn't one of those the American was seeking.

2

It was time to celebrate. The call he had just received was filled with wonderful news. And like a good Russian, the former KGB official had prepared a feast for his guests and himself. He waved at the large table covered with delicacies most Russians had forgotten existed.

"We should eat. Then we can talk some more," he suggested with a grand gesture.

The stooped nuclear scientist shook his head. "Food won't change anything."

Over the midday meal, the elderly scientist insisted on again explaining his reasons for returning to the Obrinsk Research Institute. Finally the former KGB general showed his exasperation. He pushed his forefinger into the elderly scientist's chest.

"Going back is not so simple. You endanger your friends. You endanger us."

"I have thought it through, Yuri," Polsky replied. "I will say I escaped from the kidnappers." He looked at his colleagues. "But I will add that the two of you are still captives of the men who kidnapped us."

Donielev started to get annoyed. "If that is what the professor wants to do, we must respect his wishes," he told the other two researchers.

All the three scientists knew about Donielev was that he had been with the Soviet government before he retired and that he was a friend of the woman who had introduced them to him.

What they didn't know was that the same woman had just called Yuri Donielev with exciting news.

The government had left a message on the remote-access answering machine they had set up in a small vacant office near the Arbat shopping strip.

The government was willing to pay the ransom demand for the return of the three researchers and their containers of the improved plutonium 239. All they needed were instructions on where to leave the money and where to find the missing men and containers.

The former KGB general had smiled at the news. "I thought our government was almost bankrupt. Where are they getting the money?" he had asked.

"The American government has agreed to provide the ransom. They are flying it over on a military jet. The police will meet the plane and escort two Americans accompanying the money to their embassy. By tomorrow we can set up a drop for the money."

Donielev didn't believe in taking unnecessary risks.

"The two men bringing the money, who are they?"

"According to what I've been able to learn, one of them is Harold Brognola, an older man who used to be part of the Federal Task Force on Organized Crime. He's supposed to be some kind of adviser to the American President. The second is a man named Michael Belasko. He's one of Brognola's assistants."

"Then they'll turn around and fly home?"

"Not exactly. According to my source, the reason they were asked to accompany the money was that they were coming to Russia anyway. You've heard about the big conference on fighting organized crime?"

Donielev laughed. "All the newspapers have written about how the Americans are coming here to help us get rid of the mafia. Just like they've been able to control the Mafia in their own country."

"We can talk about it over dinner," the woman said.

Donielev agreed. "I'll be starving by then. Getting rid of nuisances like this scientist always makes me hungry. I could eat a horse. Or at least a decent American steak. I'll meet you at the Exchange Restaurant, in the Radisson Slavyanskaya Hotel, at nine."

"Perhaps we should have dinner at the dacha," Kurilov suggested. "The American leader of the law-enforcement conference, Harold Brognola, is staying in the hotel."

"Isn't this Michael Belasko staying there, too?"

"No. He's in another hotel. Not one of the luxury ones."

"Can you find out anything about this Michael Belasko?"

"I tried looking in the old files. There was nothing about such a man."

The former KGB general became quiet. Then he asked, "What is the name of his hotel?"

"I don't know yet."

"Do you have a schedule on where he will be going?"

"I can get one. Why?"

"What is that American saying? An ounce of prevention is worth a kilogram of cure."

The woman laughed. "That's not exactly how the American saying goes."

"Perhaps not. But the idea is the same. Perhaps we should find out more about these men. They may become nuisances," he commented before he hung up.

PROFESSOR POLSKY LOOKED up as Donielev entered the room.

"Just remember," he reminded the scientist, "you came to us for help. Not us to you."

"I will remember and protect your identities," Polsky promised.

"And the identity of the person who introduced you to us," Donielev reminded the man.

What Polsky and his fellow scientists didn't know was that the faked kidnapping would become real. They knew about the ransom demand, but they didn't know that they were also being offered to representatives of foreign governments, or that Iran had won with a bid of thirty million dollars.

Donielev had staged the ransom demand. He had made similar demands in the past, for kidnapped businessmen, bankers and government officials. To someone, their return was obviously worth paying the ransom demands.

To make the return of the three scientists more valuable, Donielev had added another element. He had insisted that they bring with them enough of the secret plutonium 239 to make a small bomb.

"You'll see the government beg your kidnappers to return you and the plutonium," he promised the researchers.

With the thirty million from the Iranians added to the fifteen million he expected from the Russian government, Donielev and the woman could leave the bitter Russian winters behind and move to a gentler climate.

Donielev could almost feel the money in his hands, more money than he had ever seen.

The ex-KGB officer thought of the expression on the Russian president's face when he finally realized that he had been cheated. But by the time he did, the scientists would be out of the country and under lock and key at some research site in Iran.

Donielev looked at his wristwatch. He had wasted too much time trying to convince the scientist to change his mind. It was time to send Dr. Polsky on his way.

"We will drive you close enough to your institute for you to walk," he told the elderly researcher.

The goateed man stood up and hugged the other two.

"Despite your decision, I will keep your share for you against the day you decide to leave Russia for a more civilized country," Sartov promised tearfully.

Polsky cradled the plutonium container in his arms and followed Donielev out of the house.

"We are ready whenever your guest wants to leave," Viktor Shmarov, a former KGB operative and one of Donielev's key aides, announced.

A tan Volvo 750 was waiting in the driveway, its engine running.

Shmarov got in next to the driver of the car and stared disapprovingly at the blue tattoos on the back of the hardman's hands. He had tried to discourage the men from getting them. But as one of the men had explained, it was their way of bragging to their friends that they were members of one of the most powerful mafia gangs.

Donielev opened the back door and smiled at the elderly scientist. "Let me hold the container for you while you get in."

The professor handed over the lead receptacle, then got inside and looked at the seats. They were covered in plastic.

"Plastic seat covers in such a beautiful car?"

"They came from the dealer this way. I haven't had a chance to remove them yet," Donielev apologized as he shut the rear door.

"The professor is returning to the research institute in Obrinsk," Donielev told the driver. He looked at the former KGB lieutenant. "Colonel Federov told you what to do?"

The driver nodded and turned to the goateed man in the back seat. Then, steadying the silenced 9 mm Makarov autoloader on the headrest, unleashed three hollowpoints into the scientist's chest.

A stunned expression flashed over the elderly man's face as he slid down on the rear seat, blood and torn tissue from his shattered chest spattering the area.

"Clean up the mess," the square-jawed man ordered. "Make sure no one can identify him, then drive to Ismailovksy Park and bury his body in the forest."

Shmarov and the driver got out of the Volvo and headed to the garage to gather cleaning fluid, rags and a gallon bottle of acid to pour on the body after they dug a grave.

Donielev started to go back into the dacha, then stopped and signaled the other four heavyset guards to his side.

"Follow them. If anyone tries to stop them, make sure they do not live." He stared coldly at the quartet and repeated his orders. "I mean anybody—policemen, foreigners, members of other gangs. Anybody."

As both vehicles left the compound, Donielev looked down to make sure none of the scientist's blood had stained his expensive suit, then smiled and walked back into the small house.

He still had to call Haverford and work out the details about where and when to collect the ransom, and how to get the two remaining scientists to Iran.

MACK BOLAN LOOKED OUT of his window. They had been speeding along the Garden Ring, a broad boulevard that circled central Moscow. Gorsky pulled into a wide street branching off to the northeast. In the distance Bolan could see the onion roofs of a church or monastery.

"The Nikolski monastery," the Russian told him, noting the American's glance. "Famous Russian Orthodox landmark."

A huge modern stone complex stood tall and barren several streets away. Bolan recognized the buildings from previous trips. All part of the Sputnik Hotel, built in honor of the Russian cosmonauts who'd beat American astronauts early in the space race.

"We are here," the Russian announced, turning into Glavnaya Street. "Now we will search for the man."

BOLAN STOOD at the entrance to Ismailovsky Park, which was bigger than he had remembered. Dozens of makeshift stands lined the roadside that ran alongside the vast preserve. Peddlers sold everything from Polish-made umbrellas to caviar from the Caspian Sea.

Less than a dozen miles from central Moscow, the park contained more than three thousand acres of grass and a vast ancient forest. The park was a pleasant escape from the harsh reality of struggling to survive in Moscow. Lovers came here to find privacy, a haven to escape to from their crowded, tiny apartments. Families came here for a chance to smell the freshness of grass and wildflowers.

Gorsky looked at Bolan and sighed. "It is beautiful, yes?"

The American nodded.

"But like with many beautiful things, there is another side. A dangerous side," the Russian warned. "Members of the mafia come here to pursue their various deals. It's not like in the old days, when even the mafia had some honor."

He pointed to the thick woods in the distance. "Stand there at any hour of the day or night, and you will see dealers selling heroin, marijuana and such synthetic drugs like Krokodil and Chert. Big business."

Gorsky pointed out a young man in tattered clothing, wandering aimlessly nearby. "Look at his eyes."

Bolan did. There was desperation and hopelessness staring out from them. As the American watched, the young man approached another young man and whispered something. The two vanished into the woods.

"Probably a veteran of the Afghanistan war. Too many of them discovered drugs could help them forget how many people they had killed."

The former bodyguard looked discouraged.

"In this park deals for contraband goods and weapons are made. Businessmen meet with members of the various gangs to pay for protection."

He pointed to a teenage girl in a miniskirt walking quickly down a path. "She is probably meeting her pimp to get her next assignment."

From what he had read, Bolan knew that the park was also a place of death. At least four or five bodies, riddled with bullets, were discovered in Ismailovsky Park every week.

"We have a Russian expression for what is happening to this city. Unfortunately it does not translate well into English," Gorsky said.

The Russian could have spoken the expression in Russian.

Even though Mack Bolan found it useful to pretend he only understood a few words of the complex language, the American spoke Russian well.

Gorsky checked his wristwatch. "My friend should be around here someplace."

The Russian got out of the small car and stretched. Bolan followed him out.

The former bodyguard pulled a 5.45 mm PSM pistol from shoulder leather under his jacket and shoved it in a pocket.

"Wait here. I'll look for him," he said, and vanished into the woods.

A military jet had flown Brognola and Bolan to Russia, and the big man had brought an array of weapons in his carryall, most of which were locked in the trunk of Gorsky's car. For now, he had to depend on the silenced 9 mm Beretta 93-R he wore in a rigid shoulder rig, and the Applegate-Fairbairn combat knife strapped to his leg.

The knife and gun were ready for action.

So was he.

AS THEY MOVED into the woods, Gorsky mumbled a warning. "My friend has not arrived yet, but it is possible we will run into one or more mafia gangsters in the forest. They seem to prefer doing business away from the sunlight. It used to be a joke that the mafia was like another industry in your country. But in Russia the mafia controls everything. There are more than five thousand gangs throughout the Russian Federation. Here in Moscow alone, crime is controlled by more than twenty brigades, with thousands of armed thugs at their command.''

"Do you think the mafia is responsible for the kidnapping of the three scientists?'' Bolan asked.

Gorsky sighed. "It wouldn't surprise me. Nothing much does anymore.'' He looked around. "Perhaps Boris is meeting with someone on the other side of the forest. Wait here. I'll check.''

The former bodyguard vanished beyond the trees, and Bolan went back to reviewing what he had been told about the kidnapping.

It could have been planned by the mafia. They had engineered other kidnappings. But he remembered hearing how Russian professors received salaries that were less than what they needed to survive in the inflationary climate of their motherland.

He considered the notion that the missing scientists had planned their own kidnapping as a way to get the government to pay them what they thought they were worth.

Fifteen million dollars, according to Brognola.

The sounds of gunshots snapped Bolan out of his reflections. Without pausing, he darted toward the thick stand of trees.

Another shot echoed in the woods. As the Executioner passed across the tree line, he saw Andrei Gorsky lying on the ground, his pistol next to him. Before Bolan could check to see if he was still alive, he caught sight of two men running deeper into the woods.

He unleathered the Beretta and took up a two-handed shooting stance.

As if they had sensed his presence, the pair turned to face him.

Bolan aimed the Beretta at the closer of the two and unleashed a 3-round burst that drilled into his target's chest. The soldier didn't wait for the second gunner to pull the trigger of his mini-Uzi. He dived into a pile of dried leaves on his right before the second hit man could get off the first shot. Then, from his prone position, he snapped off a burst that punched into the hardman's skull between his eyes.

Aware that there could be others hiding and waiting for an opportunity to fire, Bolan quickly moved to the nearer corpse and grabbed the mini-Uzi.

Leathering the Beretta, the Executioner scanned the area. The forest was suddenly still. Only the stench of death spoiled the pastoral scene—and the smell of something acrid coming from behind a stand of trees.

Wondering what the odor was, Bolan cautiously worked his way around the trees until he came to a bizarre sight. Two dark-skinned men were emptying a large glass container into a long, shallow trench.

"It stinks," one of them complained in Russian.

"I guess those two took care of whoever was coming. Let's get out of here before somebody else shows up," the second man insisted, sounding edgy.

"Somebody has," Bolan said.

As if a pair of hornets had stung them, the surprised pair dived for the Czech-made 9 mm Model 75 autoloaders on the ground beside them. Bolan fired a measured shot at the closer gunner that ripped through the man's hand.

Screaming with pain, the hardman forced his hand around the automatic and started to bring it on target. The soldier relieved the would-be hit man of his agony with a pair of carefully placed rounds that carved their way through the man's chest and into his heart.

The second gunner, trying to take advantage of Bolan's temporary distraction, grabbed his 9 mm autoloader and fired wildly at where he thought his enemy had been a moment earlier.

The Executioner had already moved. Using a nearby tree as a shield, Bolan aimed the machine pistol at his panicked adversary and loosed a well-placed burst that punched into the frightened mobster, shoving him back until he tripped and fell into the narrow trench he and his comrade had been digging.

Two large, angry men raced from behind the trees, firing their 9 mm Russian-made Silent Assault Rifles on the run.

Quickly assessing the situation, Bolan dived at them, skidding along the damp earth. Before either man could adjust for their adversary's surprise move, the Executioner hosed them with a sustained burst from the Uzi.

Gripping the machine pistol, Bolan waited several moments before getting to his feet, then moved cautiously forward to check each of the four corpses. Too many good men had died by not making sure the enemy was really dead.

All the hardmen had one thing in common—each had blue tattoos on the backs of their hands.

Pointing the mini-Uzi at each body as he moved past it, Bolan checked for signs of life. There were none. He moved to the shallow trench, and a whiff of the odor coming up from the ground told him it was caused by superconcentrated acid.

The soldier looked into the trench. A body was partly hidden by the dead hardman who lay on top of it. The face was partially eaten away by the acid, but the Executioner could see the remains of a small gray beard on what had been the corpse's face and thin gray hair on what was left of the head.

An old man.

Bolan wondered why the six Russians were trying to destroy his identity.

He studied the body. The hands had been dipped in acid to burn away fingerprints, and acid had also been spilled on the corpse's face, leaving a gelatinous mass of tissue where once there had been human features. The mouth was partially open. Bolan saw stumps of teeth and a broken jaw-bone. Somebody had gone to a lot of trouble to make identification of the body impossible.

The soldier returned to where Gorsky had fallen. He kneeled and studied the still face of the man he had befriended. There was nothing he could do for him. Perhaps Brognola would send an anonymous donation to Gorsky's widow and children. They deserved at least that.

Bolan sensed that somebody was standing behind him.

Slipping his hand around the automatic weapon, he started to bring it around, then felt the cold muzzle of a gun pressing into the back of his neck.

He turned his head and saw two uniformed Moscow policeman. Each had a finger pressing against the trigger of the pistols they aimed at him.

Bolan released his grip on the mini-Uzi and got to his feet, locking his hands behind his head.

The first of the two officers shouted at him in Russian, and Bolan pretended he didn't understand.

Finally, his voice filled with rage, the Russian cop yelled in English, "You are under arrest."

As one of them kept Bolan covered, the other patted him down, shaking his head as he found the Beretta 93-R and the Applegate-Fairbairn combat knife.

As one of the cops shackled his hands behind his back, Bolan nearly smiled at the irony of the situation.

Twelve hours earlier he had sat in a conference room in Washington, D.C., listening as Hal Brognola tried to convince him to accompany him to Russia to help the Russians solve a problem that could affect the entire world.

Now he was their prisoner.

3

The Executioner remembered seeing the head of Stony Man Farm looking up to smile when he entered the base conference room.

"Thanks for coming," the big Fed said, and pointed to a chair next to his. "I need your input, Striker."

The nickname was a carryover from another time, when they first started working together on missions.

"Any time. What's up, Hal?"

The Justice man handed over a typed memo. "This."

Bolan scanned the words on the paper, then handed it back. "Sounds like somebody kidnapped three research scientists in Russia yesterday and wants heavy money to give them back." He shrugged. "From what I've read, it happens all the time over there."

"This isn't just about a kidnapping. We'd leave that up to the cops to handle. These aren't just three researchers. This is a special team of nuclear scientists who've developed a form of plutonium 239 that makes it safer to transport and handle. Not only have they disappeared, but so have six kilograms of the plutonium. And these three know how to assemble a small nuclear bomb around the new nuclear fuel that is light enough—and safe enough—to carry in a large suitcase."

"What do you want from me?"

"How do we get them back before somebody else gets their hands on the plutonium and on them?"

"Without doing some digging around Moscow, I don't know."

Brognola nodded. "That's what I told the President this morning." He studied the powerful-looking man sitting next to him. "Let me fill you in on my meeting in the Oval Office. When the President called me this morning and asked me to get to his office as fast as I could, I didn't know what to expect. Until he briefed me."

The Stony Man Farm chief still remembered every detail of the give-and-take dialogue the two men had.

"HAL, THREE OF RUSSIA'S top nuclear scientists have been kidnapped. Normally that would get a 'sorry to hear about your troubles' response from me. But the three missing men have developed a variation on weapons-grade fuel that can be transported in containers a fourth as thick as the ones we use. And they know how to assemble a nuclear device," the President had confided.

"The Russian president received a call from the kidnappers," he continued, "asking for fifteen million dollars in American currency for their return."

The fatigued-looking chief executive sighed. "The Russians have asked us to put up the money. I've agreed to do so if they let us participate in the manhunt. In fact you will be escorting the money to Moscow."

"My Intel says that there are a lot of leaks in the Russian government. If the kidnappers find out I'm there to help find them, we may lose the scientists and the plutonium."

The President smiled. "I may not be in your business, Hal, but give me credit for not putting your life or the lives of those Russian researchers in jeopardy. The Russian president and I worked out an explanation for your presence in Moscow.

"I'm telling the press this afternoon that the Russian government has asked us to advise them on how to handle the problem of organized crime in their country. I will also announce that one of my advisers—you—will head the American law-enforcement delegation. There's a military jet waiting for you at Andrews Air Force Base. Tomorrow representatives of other federal agencies, including the Secret Service, the FBI, the Drug Enforcement Administration and the Alcohol, Tobacco and Firearms Division of the Treasury Department, will fly over to join you.

"You'll be meeting with the top Russian and Moscow law-enforcement agencies for two or three days. That should give you enough reason for going there, without exposing our real interest."

"Can you have the money delivered to Stony Man Farm?"

The Chief Executive stared at the small, cigar-chomping man who sat in front of him.

"What are you cooking up in that devious brain of yours, Hal?"

"Nothing that would endanger the missing nuclear scientists."

The two men became silent until the head of Stony Man Farm decided to bring up a touchy subject. "I'm going to need a specialist to find the scientists while I hold the hands of the Russians," he added.

"Call Striker and get those men back before some unfriendly bunch gets their hands on them and that plutonium," the President replied.

BROGNOLA STARED at Bolan.

"It didn't take a genius to figure out who he meant by 'some unfriendly bunch'. Take your pick of North Korea, Iraq or Iran. They're about as unfriendly as they come. I need you, Mack. This isn't about some small-time dictator trying to invade a neighbor or kill his rivals. This is about the whole world being held ransom by a nuclear bomb that can be transported in a suitcase."

"I'll need wheels," Bolan said finally.

"There'll be a car waiting for you at the airport."

The soldier looked at the stack of papers in front of Brognola. "Is there any Intel on the kidnapping?"

Brognola dug through the stack of papers until he found the pages he wanted. "There's a report from the Federal Service for Counterintelligence, or FSK—the new Russian internal-security agency—that they believe the Russian mafia was involved in the kidnapping."

"No big surprise." Bolan shrugged. "Most of their mafia leaders are ex-KGB. If they know how to do anything, they certainly know how to murder and kidnap people."

Brognola handed him a photograph of a man in a KGB uniform. "His name is Yuri Donielev, a former major-general in charge of the Second Directorate. He had quite a reputation and is said to be a prime shaker and mover."

Bolan's eyes grew hard and cold. He had never met the man, but he knew of the horrors that the former head of the Second Directorate—the KGB division that ran internal counterintelligence—had inflicted on his victims. Bolan had tried to take him out during a previous mission, but Donielev had escaped while other KGB department heads had died at the hands of the Executioner. This was the first time he had heard Donielev's name mentioned since he'd been dismissed from the secret police.

Hal Brognola filled him in on what his sources knew about the ex-KGB general. "He claims he's a partner in a lot of different businesses, like real estate, nightclubs, gambling casinos. All that clean stuff. But some of the FSK's staff believes his real money comes from being the godfather of one of the more violent mafia gangs in Moscow. According to the Russians, Donielev has been involved in other kidnappings. But until now the victims have been bankers or rich businessmen."

"The kidnapping sounds like something Donielev might set up."

"Some of our people aren't much better."

"Like who?"

Brognola handed him another photograph. "This is ten years old, part of the official CIA personnel files."

Bolan studied the picture of a well-dressed man with long, stylishly trimmed hair. There was a haughtiness in his expression, often seen in those born to money and position.

"Max Haverford."

The Executioner quickly sorted through the banks of information stored in his brain. "Central Intelligence Agency. Used to run the Eastern Europe desk in Langley. I remember hearing about him."

"He was a pretty nasty customer in his day."

"As I remember, Haverford had a reputation for hiring more contract hit men than anybody else in the Agency. Didn't he get canned for knocking off suspects without approval from upstairs?"

"Technically he's retired and running an international consulting firm with offices in major cities around the world."

"What's Haverford got to do with the kidnappings?" Bolan asked.

"On the surface, nothing. But word from our friends in the *mujahedin* movement is that he's been meeting with Deputy Intelligence Minister Massoud Yaneri for the past week."

Brognola started to hand his friend another photograph.

"I know what he looks like," Bolan replied, rejecting the picture.

Bolan remembered Yaneri from the time the Iranian VEVAK secret-police official was in charge of the assassination of dissidents hiding in foreign countries. He had ordered the murder of former Iranian Prime Minister Shahpour Bakhtiar in Paris, the death of Kassem Rajavi, spokesman for the *mujahedin* to the UN Commission on Human Rights in Geneva, the machine-gun killing of Iranian dissident Parvis Dasmalchi in Berlin, Iranian Kurd leader Abdelrahman Qassemlou's assassination in Vienna and a dozen other murders in foreign countries.

According to Intel reports, Yaneri had been promoted to deputy minister by Mullah Fallahian, the Iranian Intelligence minister, and personally handled only the most sensitive situations.

"Haverford's meeting with the new deputy minister means he's got something the Iranians want badly. And what could they want more than nuclear experts and enough of the new version of plutonium 239 to manufacture a small, easily transportable bomb."

"Those three need to be retired permanently."

"I agree," Brognola replied. "Just don't forget Haverford went to the same Ivy League schools as some of the CIA top brass, which means he doesn't leave a smell when he goes to the bathroom.

"And the reason we're going to Russia," Brognola reminded him, "is to get back the scientists and the plutonium. If some nut case like Yaneri gets the nuclear specialists and their plutonium, you'll see hard-liners in Russia and in our country coming out of the woodwork, trying to blame each other for the theft. And then, there goes the ballgame. We're back to the days of the cold war."

As Bolan knew, the cold war was almost back. Activists from the old Communist leadership were trying to stir up people with promises of a better life when they came back into power. They insisted that Russia should again treat the United States like their mortal enemy. The far-right back in the States was preaching the same message and starting to find ears willing to listen.

Losing one of their prized top secrets and the men who were responsible might be enough to tumble the present government and put the hard-liners back in charge.

Bolan drummed his fingers on the table, thinking over the situation.

"As much as I desperately need you, I can't give you much hands-on help with this one," Brognola stated. "The Russians have offered to cooperate in every way they can. They can't afford to let the story get to the press."

Bolan looked directly into Brognola's eyes.

"When are you leaving?"

"Hopefully in an hour. As soon as an armored truck from Stony Man Farm arrives," Brognola answered.

"Armored car?"

The big Fed boss dodged the question. "I'll tell you about that later. Right now I need your answer."

The Executioner pulled himself to his feet, then walked to the door and opened it. "You can brief me on the other details when we're in the air."

4

The small suite of offices on the second floor of the Radisson Slavyanskaya Hotel was tastefully furnished with furniture imported from Copenhagen.

The understated engraved-metal square mounted on the front door announced that this was the entrance to one of the offices of Maxwell Haverford Associates, Business Consultants. Beneath the name were the cities in which they had facilities: Washington, D.C., Zurich, Beirut, Hong Kong and Moscow.

Inside, a handsome Russian woman in her late thirties sat behind the oak desk in the reception area, typing correspondence on a computer keyboard. Her desk drawer was partially open. Sitting in it, ready to be fired, was a 9 mm Makarov autoloader, fitted with a bulky silencer.

The intercom buzzed.

"Yes, Mr. Haverford?" she said, answering it.

"Is Gilal in?"

"Yes, he's in his office."

"Have him join me," Haverford ordered.

INSIDE ONE of the smaller offices, a heavyset man with a crew cut was finishing a telephone conversation when the intercom buzzed.

"He wants to see you," the woman said.

Gilal Kurbanov gathered up the reports and stopped at the receptionist's desk. Looking concerned, he asked, "Any idea what he wants?"

"No," she replied, then looked at the lights on the multi-button phone. "He is on an international call, but he said for you to go into his office."

"I have an offer. From Baghdad," Kurbanov confided.

The handsome woman beamed. "Congratulations. Isn't this much better than the old days on Dzerzhinksy Square?"

"It wasn't like that in Azerbaijan," Kurbanov interjected. "But the Azeris are all crazy. They were like American cowboys. Always shooting off guns, at anything and anyone. For a bunch of Muslims, they either drank too much or used too many drugs. Or both."

The woman stared at him with contempt. "You are an Azeri. Is that how you talk about your own people?"

Kurbanov looked offended. "I am not an Azeri. My family are Talysh. We can trace our history back two thousand years."

The intercom buzzed again.

She looked at the man. "He's getting impatient."

HAVERFORD'S LARGE OFFICE was a copy of the Oval Office of the White House. Perfect copies of its antique furniture filled the room. The easy chairs and couch were covered with duplicates of the Oval Office fabrics.

Sitting behind the large desk, Haverford toyed with a gold pencil as he continued to listen to the voice on the other end of the line. He'd done nothing but listen for the past twenty minutes. Yaneri, the Iranian deputy Intelligence minister, loved to lecture on why his country was chosen to save the world from the Great Satan, as he called the United States, and its demon brothers.

The door opened, and Haverford waved Kurbanov into the room, pointing to a seat near his desk.

While his assistant sat, Haverford decided to interrupt. "I understand your point of view, Mr. Yaneri. But let's get down to business. Do you want the two men and their samples?"

"When we first spoke, you said there would be three experts," Yaneri reminded him.

"One of them met with a tragic accident. But the other two have been the key scientists responsible for constructing the devices for their country."

Haverford asked the caller to hold for a moment, then covered the mouthpiece and looked at Kurbanov. "Any word from the other governments?"

"Baghdad will pay ten million. But first they want to make sure the men are the experts I represented them to be," Kurbanov reported. "No reply from North Korea yet."

Haverford nodded. It was what he expected to hear. "If you've changed your mind, we do have offers from several other governments," he told the caller.

"How much were you asking?"

"Forty million in American dollars."

Yaneri exploded. "Robbery! We are a poor country."

"Who wants to survive in a hostile world," Haverford replied.

"We'll pay no more than thirty million."

"All right, since we've done business before. But remember, we aren't bargaining for a Persian rug. If you can get the same help elsewhere for less money, please do so."

One long minute of silence greeted the ex-CIA agent's reply.

Then Yaneri spoke. "We have a deal," he said in defeat. "Where and when?"

"In Baku. We'll call you with the exact location to make the trade. As far as when, we're planning to fly there within the next twenty-four to thirty-six hours."

The Iranian offered an alternative plan. "Fly them to Rasht. It's just across the Caspian Sea. We can make the trade there."

"Baku," Haverford insisted.

"You don't trust us," Yaneri complained.

"You've been in our country, haven't you?"

Yaneri was puzzled. "Yes. So what?"

"We have an expression. Better safe than sorry." The American paused, then added, "I'll call you when we get into Baku."

"Baku. A filthy city. So unlike Rasht."

"At least all of us will leave there alive," Haverford replied, then hung up the phone.

He turned to his assistant. "I need several places where I can store the two men until the deal is closed. Got any ideas?"

Kurbanov thought for a moment. "I can borrow a farm in the foothills overlooking Baku. The owner retired from the KGB down there and is always willing to rent his place, if the price is right."

"Does it come with guards?"

"He can get them. Good men. Former KGB field operatives and Vysotniki troopers, now hiring themselves out as mercenaries."

"How about some safe place I can meet with the Iranians and work out the details of the exchange? I don't want them to know where the two researchers are until after we collect the money."

Kurbanov shuffled through the lists of contacts he had in Baku. Suddenly he lifted his head, smiling. "I know the perfect place. A small industrial warehouse in the factory district of Baku. The owner is an Armenian who pretends he is an Azeri."

Haverford was aware of the bloody battles between the Azeris and the Armenians. Blood feuds between them had lasted for a thousand years. Hate ran deep along the Caspian Sea.

"I may need another place—more remote—in case Yaneri starts making the wrong kind of moves."

"Leave it to me. I have an uncle in the village of Palikesh. It's in the Talysh Mountains and difficult to get to except by helicopter. I'm sure he wouldn't turn down his favorite nephew."

Haverford smiled, then asked, "Do you have an alternate in the unlikely event he does?"

Kurbanov's expression hardened. "He won't. Not if he wants his beautiful sixteen-year-old daughter to live," he replied ominously.

HAL BROGNOLA FELT uncomfortable sitting at the large oak table. The room in which the conference was taking place was huge, and was crowded with old paintings from the collection of the Hermitage Museum, in St. Petersburg.

A large baize cloth covered the long table. Cups of tea and small bottles of mineral water sat next to large crystal ashtrays in front of each of the huge oak armchairs that surrounded the conference table.

Five men and one woman, all dressed in military style uniforms, stared at the hard-faced American. All of them had at least one aide seated behind them.

Brognola had met all of them at a brief ceremony. On his right sat General Nicolai Podkin, deputy director of the newly formed FSK, which was responsible for internal security in Russia, a function once handled by the KGB.

Next to him sat Major-General Dimitri Droschinskaya, a gray-haired senior member of the SVR—the Russian Foreign Intelligence Service—which had replaced the KGB's international spy operations. The Stony Man Farm chief could only surmise that Droschinskaya was present because of alliances the various gangs of the Russian mafia had made with their counterpart in Italy and the United States.

Vladimir Brushnikov, head of the Sixth Department of the Interior Ministry, which was responsible for fighting organized crime throughout the Russian Federation, faced him from across the table. Next to Brushnikov sat General Boris Gurov, head of the Moscow Police Special Crimes Unit, which was faced with the task of dealing with the thousands of mafia mobsters who preyed on both residents and Western visitors.

At the far end of the table sat Viktor Lasky, a Russian presidential aide. Brognola's Intel had contained a brief background on the neatly dressed young man.

A graduate of the London School of Economics, the thirty-three-year-old official was responsible for coordinating efforts to rid the Russian Federation of criminal elements who stopped foreign businessmen from investing money in the country.

The only item in the report that bothered Brognola was the comment that Viktor Lasky lived well for someone on a government salary.

"Officially you are here to advise my government on how to eliminate the problem of the *mafiya,* as we call it here," Lasky said to Brognola. "Will you have others at the conferences tomorrow?"

"Several senior FBI officials, a representative of the Drug Enforcement Administration and three officials from the Treasury Department—one from the unit responsible for the safety of our President, another from the group that concerns itself with counterfeiting and one from the division that deals with alcohol, tobacco and firearms problems—should arrive this evening. They'll join us at tomorrow's meetings."

"All of the issues these men deal with are serious problems Russia faces today," said the redheaded woman in a colonel's uniform who sat at the far end of the table. "We have others, as well."

The other Russians at the table turned and glared at her. "We don't have to discuss issues that are not the concern of a guest to our country," the deputy director of the internal-security agency snapped in admonishment.

Lasky scowled at the redheaded colonel and turned to Brognola. "And of course there is Mr. Belasko. I understand that he has an interesting background."

Brognola toyed with the unlit cigar he held in his right hand. He needed a moment to formulate a reply.

"Michael Belasko has been a very valuable asset to the Justice Department. Because of the sensitive nature of his work, he avoids any publicity."

"He must have a philosophy under which he functions," the Moscow police official commented.

"He does," the Stony Man Farm chief replied. "A direct threat requires direct action. If you're attacked by a rabid dog, you don't try to reason with it. You kill it."

Nobody at the conference table was willing to offer a comment. Finally the attractive redheaded colonel smiled. "It is difficult to bite the hand that feeds you," she said cryptically.

She ignored the angry looks from the others in the room and turned to the young dark-haired female lieutenant who sat directly behind her. "Did you bring the latest press estimates on how many public officials have let themselves be compromised by accepting *gifts?*"

Lieutenant Lena Kurilov opened the thick briefcase she carried and reached inside.

"No need," Brognola commented.

Tolstoy's uniformed aide looked at the colonel, who held up a hand to stop her.

Brognola liked the woman's frankness. The head Fed was aware of the widespread corruption among government officials.

The room became painfully quiet.

Hal Brognola decided to break the silence. "Any questions before we break up?"

He looked around the room. Each of the men seemed afraid that any questions they might ask him would make them look stupid. Finally his eyes stopped at the flame-haired colonel.

"Rumor has it that you are the head of an interesting unit of your government," she commented. "Too bad you couldn't bring others of your organization. I'm certain they would have been very interesting."

Brognola swallowed hard. The colonel was a ballsy lady—maybe a little too ballsy.

When Lasky had introduced them at the reception before the conference, her name, Irina Tolstoy, was familiar to him. Five years earlier, as a major in the KGB, the woman had worked with some members of Phoenix Force to find and destroy people who were trying to cripple the American-Russian agreement to dismantle their nuclear missiles.

General Podkin broke the silence with a question. "Since you are the expert on the American Mafia, Mr. Brognola, how do you suggest we deal with the problem of organized crime?"

Hal Brognola studied the man as he tried to frame a response. "I'd rather let Mr. Belasko's philosophy stand as my answer."

The head Fed wondered how the group at the table would react if they knew that consultant Michael Belasko was the notorious Mack Bolan, for whom the KGB, until it was shut down, had a standing execution order. He had been responsible for the deaths of many of their field operatives and senior officials.

"We would like to hear your opinion," the FSK deputy director insisted.

Brognola looked at the faces around the table. They were waiting for his answer.

"The way to deal with the Mafia is to wipe them out," he replied.

General Boris Gurov looked surprised. "You mean kill them?"

"Yes."

"Is that how you handle the Mafia in your country?" Tolstoy asked.

"As often as we can," he replied. "We have a special problem. The Mafia in our country has made deep inroads among government officials and into the political and judiciary system."

Tolstoy continued her questioning. "You mean they own politicians and judges?"

"Yes."

The woman looked at the faces of the others at the table, then said, "So do ours. And we have a special problem you don't seem to have."

Ignoring the angry stares of the other Russians at the table, she continued. "Many of the mafia leaders in Russia and the other former Soviet republics are former KGB."

Still ignoring the angry glares from the men at the table, she added, "The unemployment rate among former KGB employees is extremely high. I should know. I was one of them until the Ministry of Atomic Energy asked me to join them.

"A KGB employee, even senior staff, receives an average of thirty dollars a month in pensions. Even the former head of the Soviet Union receives a pension of less than five hundred dollars a month, and he survives on the fees he is paid for lectures he gives abroad. It is no wonder that many of them turn to organized crime."

The head Fed nodded his understanding and turned to the senior Moscow police official. "How bad is the organized-crime situation here in Moscow?"

"Last year at least five thousand murders were committed by mafia gangs. It has gotten so bad that anybody opening a new business makes the first call to the mafia to purchase protection."

The door opened, and a young uniformed officer entered. He moved quickly to Gurov's side and whispered into his ear. The general nodded, then turned to the group and apologized.

"An important call has just come in. I will be right back."

He rose and followed the young officer out of the conference room.

A few minutes later Gurov returned. "There seems to be a problem," he said to Brognola. "A number of citizens have been found dead. Your Michael Belasko is being held at police headquarters for the killings."

"I'll go and get this straightened out," Brognola insisted, pushing back his chair and standing.

"So will I," Tolstoy added.

"This is a matter for the Moscow police," General Gurov sternly reminded them.

"Not if the Russians want our help," Brognola snapped as he walked out of the conference room, followed by Colonel Tolstoy and the young woman who served as her aide.

DONIELEV CLENCHED a fist and forcibly had to restrain himself from ramming it into the face of the nervous young man who had brought him the news. Leon Mosheyev wasn't surprised at the barely leashed anger. He had worked for the general in the KGB as his secretary.

"What do you mean dead? All six of them?" He showed his rage, smashing his hand on the antique table in the dacha's living room. "How many police showed up in the park?"

Almost stuttering, the news bearer replied, "It was the other man who shot them."

The former KGB major-general grabbed Mosheyev by his jacket collar and pulled him closer. "What man, Leon?"

"An American, General. According to our contact at police headquarters, his name is Mikhail Belasko."

What kind of man was this Belasko? For some reason he reminded the former KGB director of another man, a man they called the Executioner.

But that man was dead. It was a well-known fact. He had been killed in a battle. Unfortunately not before he had murdered almost the entire senior staff of the KGB. Donielev would have been among the dead if he hadn't slipped out of the conference room where the confrontation had taken place to smoke a cigarette.

Now this Belasko appeared, another skilled killer, like the man he had succeeded. Donielev wondered if the Americans had some secret training site where they developed such men. And if they did have one, why had none of the KGB's agents ever found it?

There was nothing he could do about the dead street soldiers. But there was the matter of honor. Such a crime couldn't go unpunished.

5

Petrograv 99—the headquarters of the Moscow police—looked like police headquarters all around the world: long, dingy hallways, and chipped and stained ancient furniture.

To the bored-looking police sergeant behind the elevated front desk, Mack Bolan was no different than any other criminal who stood before him. He shouted at the handcuffed man in Russian, but Bolan pretended he didn't understand. The sergeant looked at the two arresting officers, one of whom quickly explained that they had found Bolan standing over the bodies.

"Americanski," one of them explained.

The desk officer then turned to Bolan. In broken English he asked, "Do you understand why you are here?"

Bolan shook his head.

"You are here because you killed six innocent citizens. And perhaps you also are responsible for the death of the citizen who lay in the shallow grave! In Russia murderers are put to death. Not like in your country, where some clever lawyer lets them escape punishment!"

Bolan knew that trying to explain what had happened was useless. The Russian behind the desk had already convicted him.

The sergeant turned to one of the two uniformed cops. "Take him to the laboratory for photographs and fingerprints," he ordered.

BOLAN'S STEPS ECHOED as he left the crime lab and walked down the long corridor filled with barred cells. A sour-faced guard opened a heavy metal door and shoved him into the small room.

A narrow metal bed was attached to the wall, and a small metal stool was firmly bolted to the floor next to a malodorous toilet. A small bulb, protected from breakage by a grilled shield, filled the area with weak light.

The Executioner examined his surroundings. Compared to this, he suspected even the most primitive of American jails looked modern. There was no way he could escape. All he could do was to wait for Brognola to bail him out—if he even knew Bolan had been arrested.

Sitting on the small stool, Bolan thought about his conversation with Brognola on the flight from the United States.

THEY HAD BEEN the only passengers on the military jet winging its way to Moscow. Bolan sat next to Brognola and listened as the man provided more information on the kidnappings.

"As I mentioned, we put up the cash for the ransom," the big Fed head had said.

"I don't agree with encouraging kidnapping by giving in to the demands."

"You can tell them that when you see them," Brognola had commented.

He pointed to a stack of metal cases in the rear of the cabin.

"The money is in those cases, and you're going to help deliver the money personally to the kidnappers as soon as they tell us where and when. Just don't decide to open the cases and examine the money."

Bolan knew Brognola had a fifth ace up his sleeve.

"What's wrong with it? Counterfeit?"

"No, it's legitimate. But I think the kidnappers are going to find it too hot to handle. It's been treated."

Leaning back in his seat, Bolan could feel the silenced Beretta 93-R pressing against his shoulder. The powerful autoloader was sitting in a rigid holster under his jacket. Strapped to his thigh was an Applegate-Fairbairn double-edge combat knife, perfect for close-in fighting. An assortment of other weapons was stashed in a carryall that lay at his feet.

"That doesn't look like Sheremetyevo II Airport below us," he commented.

"We're landing at Vnukovo Airport instead. The Russians thought it would be smarter to bring us in at one of the smaller domestic airports, where there aren't so many curious bystanders," Brognola explained.

After landing, the pair left the military jet and, led by an airport official, walked down a wide corridor past customs.

A smiling young man in an American-style business suit stopped Bolan and Brognola at the end of the hallway.

"Welcome to Russia," he said with a grin, first grabbing Brognola's hand and shaking it, then repeating the gesture with Bolan. "I am Viktor Lasky, one of the president's aides. He has sent me to help deliver you to your hotels."

Brognola looked back at the plane. Three of the jet's crew were struggling to unload the metal containers onto a motorized luggage carrier.

"We have to make a quick stop at the American Embassy first," he said.

"No problem," Lasky replied. "I am aware of your cargo." He pointed to a GMC panel truck, with the United States symbol painted on its door. Eight uniformed Moscow police officers stood near it. "With your permission, we will make sure it is delivered safely to your embassy vault."

He handed the two men typewritten pages. "These are your itineraries," he said, still working overtime to be charming.

"All I want is to get to my hotel and take a nap," Brognola growled. He looked at Bolan. "Want to change your mind and move to my hotel? It's supposed to be one of the best in Moscow."

Bolan hadn't come to sample Moscow hospitality.

"No, thanks. The Radisson is reserved for big shots, not little guys like me," he replied with a smile.

Bolan handed back the itinerary to the presidential aide. "I've made my own arrangements," he said.

Brognola looked at Bolan. "Meet me at my hotel right after you finish with what you've got planned."

"Why?"

"You'll get to meet the Russian guide who's been lined up for you."

Bolan grunted. The one thing he didn't need was some fawning government aide hanging around.

"I think you'll like her. She's part of the security force at the Ministry of Atomic Energy. And she's been successful at recovering stolen plutonium and uranium, according to the Russians in their Washington embassy."

"Does she speak English?"

"Yeah, she does. And with a Californian accent. She got her advanced degree as an exchange student at Cal Tech."

Brognola turned and walked back to the waiting limousine before he could be asked any more questions.

A SOBER-FACED WOMAN in a police uniform approached Bolan's cell, then turned to the two Moscow cops who had accompanied her. "General Yorsky wants him in his office."

The pair of officers looked at each other and hesitated.

"Now," she insisted.

GENERAL MAXIM YORSKY had been with the Moscow police for over forty years. Under the Stalinist regime he had joined the force and worked his way up through the ranks. Unlike many of the others, he had successfully avoided becoming an informer for the NKVD—the Intelligence agency that preceded the KGB—in exchange for promotions.

Somehow he had managed to avoid getting involved in the complex games the KGB played until its demise. Others in the police department hadn't been so fortunate. Most—not all—had been dismissed when the KGB was disbanded.

Yorksy wasn't naive. He knew that those who had avoided being fired were still informants for their former KGB employers. But since the ex-KGB officials now were part of the network of Russian mafia gangs, they still had a pipeline into the confidential files of the Moscow police.

Someone knocked on his office door.

"Enter."

The door opened, and Maria Ospenskaya, the uniformed officer who functioned as his aide and secretary, looked at him from the hallway. "The two arresting officers are here with the prisoner," she said.

"Bring him in."

She turned and gave a signal before vanishing.

Bolan was led into the large, plainly furnished room by the two officers.

Yorsky looked at him. The American was larger than he had expected. He could understand why this man could deal effectively with the Mafia in America, as he had learned from the phone call he had received from Viktor Lasky.

"Take his handcuffs off," he ordered.

The two officers looked puzzled but didn't question the order. Keeping their guns drawn, they removed the cuffs from Bolan's wrists, then pulled back and waited.

Yorsky pointed to a chair at the side of the desk. "Sit down," he said softly.

The soldier looked surprised but eased into the chair.

"One of the men was killed by bullets from a Skorpion submachine gun," Yorsky said to the officers. "The other six—the men the American shot—are all wanted for murder. Criminals," he snapped. "Not innocent citizens."

One of the officers protested. "What about the partially destroyed body we found?"

Yorsky shook his head. "Somebody poured acid on his face and hands to delay identification. They also smashed his teeth so dental records would be difficult to check. The only thing we found on him was a tattoo of numbers on his forearm. And, according to the pathologist, a low level of radiation from exposure to some nuclear materials."

The police official stared at Bolan, then turned back to the officers. "Return his weapons to him before he leaves."

He turned to Bolan. "We owe you an apology, Mr. Belasko."

Yorsky then looked at the two officers. "Don't we?"

Both uniformed men looked embarrassed. Finally one of them spoke. "I suppose so." Humiliated, he shook his head, avoiding eye contact with Bolan. "How were we to know?"

HAL BROGNOLA EXPECTED to find Bolan locked in a dark basement cell. Anxious because he thought the soldier might have suffered at the hands of the Moscow police, the big Fed stormed past his escorts and tore open the door to the deputy police chief's office, closely followed by General Gurov and Irina Tolstoy.

He stopped short when he saw Mack Bolan and the uniformed man behind the desk laughing. The Executioner had the leather rig holding the Beretta 93-R slung over a shoulder. He was nodding as the uniformed man behind the desk made a comment.

"I apologize for inconveniencing you, Mr. Belasko."

The soldier was about to say something when he looked up and saw Brognola.

"We've got work to do," Brognola growled, masking his relief at finding Bolan alive.

6

"I want Belasko dead," Donielev shouted. "I don't care how many men it takes!"

He needed to take immediate action before any of the other gangs heard about the killings. This could be the opening they needed to declare open season on his men.

"I assume the American government got him released from police headquarters."

"Yes. Some American official came and picked him up." The young man paused, then added, "There was a woman with the American official, according to our contact."

"From the American Embassy?"

"She wore a Russian uniform. A colonel. He described her. She had bright red hair—"

Donielev held up a hand. "I know her."

Too well. Of all the women he'd known, she was the only one who had ever refused him. Others begged to join him in his bed, but not her. Once, when they had left a KGB party at the same time, both drunk, he had given her a lift home and forced his way into her apartment. Before he could push her down on her bed, she had shoved a small automatic pistol against his right eye and threatened to kill him if he didn't leave immediately.

The only comfort he had was his belief that the woman was secretly a lesbian. Otherwise she wouldn't have kept turning him down. Now Irina Tolstoy—*Colonel* Irina Tolstoy, he reminded himself—was working with the Americans. And against him. He had monitored her actions from reports Lena Kurilov had given him.

She should also be eliminated. But not yet.

The death of an American visitor was one thing. The death of someone with Tolstoy's connections might lead to a study of her KGB files. He was certain she had filed reports about him with the agency. He had never been permitted to read his files, even when he threatened the keepers of the records.

Now that he was no longer with the government, he would never find out what the KGB—or its successors—knew about him.

He stared at the young messenger. "Did the contact say where they were going?"

"He overheard them talking about having a meeting at the Radisson Slavyanskaya Hotel."

The young man started to leave, then stopped. "Should I tell Colonel Federov you wish to see him?"

Donielev nodded.

When the crew-cut ex-KGB officer came into the room, Donielev was leaning back in an easy chair, his eyes closed, listening to classical music being played on the American stereo system he had imported.

Snapping to attention, Federov waited for the general to speak.

"The young people don't appreciate good music. All they care about is that trash—that rock-and-roll noise," the mafia leader commented, his eyes still closed.

"Yes, sir." The former colonel had been with the general for enough years to know that his superior wouldn't be rushed into saying anything before he was ready.

Five minutes passed, then Donielev opened his eyes and turned off the stereo. He turned and studied his long-time assistant. "We have been together for many years, Vasily."

"Yes, sir."

"You have been of great assistance to me many times. I want you to know I am grateful."

Federov glanced at his superior. Was General Donielev becoming senile and sentimental?

"We have a problem. An American has murdered six good men."

"I heard. If I had been there, the results would have been different."

"I believe that, which is why I want you to personally handle a special mission."

He told about the meeting at the Radisson Slavyanskaya Hotel.

"When he leaves, I would like two police officers to chase him and kill him. They thought he was an American criminal, especially when he wouldn't stop the car he was driving."

"Are you sure he won't be taking a cab?"

"One of the hotel garage attendants told one of our men that a Volga had been parked in the garage by someone at the American Embassy, with orders to turn it over to Michael Belasko."

Federov had a suggestion. "We could wire a bomb to the car's ignition."

"Good thinking. But no. The embassy has stationed a guard at the car until this Belasko picks it up."

Donielev saw the sudden gleam in his aide's eyes. "We don't want to declare war on the United States. We just want to kill Belasko," he cautioned.

The gleam faded.

"Will the woman colonel be traveling with him?"

"If she is, have whoever chases his car find a way to spare her life."

He saw the puzzled expression on the man's face.

"That is an order."

The colonel saluted and turned to leave. Then, at the doorway, he stopped and said, "I presume it would be acceptable if I arranged for our men to provide backup in case the police car can't catch the American.''

''Of course, Vasily. What did you have in mind?''

''We have a number of those BTR-40 Armored Personnel Carriers in storage at the weapons warehouse. Until we sell them, they are just sitting there, useless. I would like to select the men for this mission.''

''Approved.''

Federov vanished from the doorway.

Donielev was satisfied. The colonel was always thorough. Before the evening was over, the American would be having dinner with the devil.

WHILE COLONEL TOLSTOY used the telephone in Brognola's hotel room, her young aide at her side, the big Fed leaned over and handed Bolan a parking receipt.

''There's a car parked in the garage so you can move around the area. It's one of those Russian-made jobs, a Volga.''

''Not much power if I have to move fast,'' Bolan commented.

''Don't worry about it. This one's been worked on by an American mechanic who thinks it's going to be competing in the Indianapolis 500.

''By the way, how did you get out of the jam?''

''They found tattoos on the six corpses,'' Bolan replied.

Tolstoy hung up the phone and joined the two men. Lowering herself into an upholstered chair, she listened to Brognola.

''Tattoos?'' The Stony Man Farm chief was perplexed. ''What the hell have tattoos got to do with anything?''

The Russian colonel started to explain when her aide interrupted.

''If you don't have any need for me, Colonel . . .''

''No, you've already put in more than a full day, Lena. If you can wait, I'll drive you home.''

"My grandmother is probably exhausted from playing with my daughter. I'd better leave. But I can call a friend. I'm sure he'll pick me up."

Tolstoy nodded, and the young lieutenant turned and left the suite.

After the door had closed, Tolstoy turned to Brognola. "Perhaps I can explain. Most of the members of the various mafia groups wear tattoos. Especially on the backs of their hands. They have them done in prison, then show them off so everyone knows they are part of an important gang." She turned to Bolan. "You know there were eight bodies found. The eighth body should interest you, Mr. Belasko.

"Despite efforts to destroy his identity, the forensic doctors found an old tattoo on his forearm. A set of numbers crudely burned into the corpse's flesh. As a child Professor Aleksander Polsky had been in the Auschwitz concentration camp. The tattoo was part of his official record."

The Executioner knew the old man had been through enough without the final degradation of denying him his identity. "Any sign of the other two scientists?"

She shook her head. "Not yet. But I have some background information you should know. There was a young man employed at the Obrinsk Research Institute who had been suspected of stealing nuclear materials in the past. His name was Oleg Aliyev.

"I had interrogated him. He finally admitted that he had arranged for the three scientists to be driven to a small restaurant on the outskirts of the city."

"At gunpoint?"

"Voluntarily."

"Good work, Colonel," Bolan commented. "What will happen to this Aliyev?"

"He is dead."

Bolan stared at the woman. Had she ordered him killed?

"One of the criminals he chose to associate with must have killed him," she added. "He would have gone to prison if he had lived." Her voice had a hard edge to it.

"You sound like it's more than another criminal matter."

"It is. The young man was my late sister's oldest child— my nephew. I had gotten him the job," she said, not bothering to hide the anger in her voice.

"And," she added bitterly, "even in death, I hold him personally responsible for the murder of Professor Polsky."

Silence filled the hotel room. Finally the woman stood. "It is time for me to leave. I have a small gift for you."

She reached into the bulky handbag she carried and withdrew papers. Handing them to Bolan, she commented, "You might like the return of these."

Bolan looked at the documents: a set of fingerprints and his police photographs.

"Thanks. How'd you get these?"

"Something I learned when I was in your country. RHIP," she replied lightly. "Come visit me at my office. I can fill you in on everything we know about the situation with the missing scientists."

Bolan got to his feet. "At the Ministry of Atomic Energy?"

She smiled and shook her head. "A much more historic building. The former KGB headquarters on what used to be called Dzerzhinsky Square. I suspect you know where that is."

Still smiling, she left the hotel room and a speechless Mack Bolan.

Brognola laughed. "Talk about Daniel and the lion's den."

"More like volunteering to jump into a pit filled with rattlesnakes," Bolan replied.

"You going to beg off?"

"No," the soldier replied, then stood and checked the weapons he was carrying. "I'm curious to see if any of the pit vipers still work there."

As he turned to leave, Brognola stopped him.

"What the hell is RHIP?"

"You of all people should know," Bolan replied. "Rank has its privileges."

7

Bolan was surprised to see Irina Tolstoy in the lobby of Brognola's hotel. She was talking into a pay phone, but hung up abruptly when she saw him coming toward her.

"I thought you left."

"I decided to check if anyone has heard from the kidnappers."

"Did they?"

She nodded. "A letter was delivered to the president's office by a young boy. Someone had stopped him on the street and gave him some money to deliver an envelope."

"Any fix on the man who paid him?"

"The boy spent the day going through books of pictures of known criminals but couldn't find one of the man," she replied.

"What was in the letter?"

"A place to leave the money was named. A Moscow park. Sokolniki. An hour after the money's dropped the president's office will get a call telling where the nuclear experts and their plutonium can be found. The letter swore the men would still be alive."

"When does this all happen?"

Tolstoy looked concerned. "Tomorrow night at ten. Perhaps we should talk briefly about the mission before I go home."

"We could do that tomorrow morning when we meet," Bolan suggested.

"My office may have more ears than mine. Even though I have it checked almost daily, one doesn't know who has installed listening devices. I will have it checked before your arrival tomorrow."

Bolan saw a bar across the lobby. "Let's have a drink while we talk."

"Good. Then I can drop you at your hotel before I drive home."

"No need. I've got my own transportation," Bolan replied.

From the doorway the soldier saw an empty pair of upholstered easy chairs in a corner. A waiter approached them. Bolan pointed to the vacant seats and followed Tolstoy as she led the way.

While Bolan ordered a stein of imported beer, the colonel ordered a bottle of wine. She let the waiter pour the first glass.

"To success," she said, lifting the glass.

"And survival," Bolan replied, touching her glass with his mug.

She studied the big American with the intense eyes for a moment, then took another sip. "I am not sure that what we have here is a true kidnapping," she commented in a low voice.

That was what he thought, and he was curious why she thought so, too. "What makes you say that?"

"For one thing the testimony of my nephew. He said the three scientists approached him to introduce them to someone who could make their disappearance look like a kidnapping."

"Did he say who he introduced them to?"

"A woman who had connections, was all he would say. I got the impression he was having an affair with her."

"Why do you think the scientists would want to fake their own kidnapping?"

"Like everybody else who holds an honest job in Russia, scientists are poorly paid. What would be better than sharing a prize of fifteen million dollars, in American currency, for their return?"

"Who did the men finally meet?"

"A man who dealt in the black market. A former KGB officer, Viktor Shmarov. He was once a lieutenant on the staff of KGB General Yuri Donielev." She paused. "He was one of the six men you shot in the park."

"If Donielev is involved, I can't see him returning the scientists. Under pressure they would crack and implicate him."

"It's not his style," she agreed.

The soldier posed a question. "What happens to the scientists and the plutonium if the money is collected and the experts and the plutonium aren't delivered?"

"Probably they will be killed or sold to the highest bidder."

"Exactly. Probably to Iraq, North Korea or Iran."

"It would have to be one of them," she agreed. "They have the desire to manufacture a bomb, and they could use the skills of trained nuclear specialists."

Bolan knew something about how nuclear bombs were constructed, but not as much as someone like Irina Tolstoy.

"How much expertise is needed?"

"More than I have. The six kilograms of plutonium that is missing is sufficient to manufacture a small bomb, providing you know what you are doing. First of all, the plutonium the scientists took was in bar form."

"I'm surprised the three men didn't get radiation poisoning."

"Plutonium does not emit deep alpha rays." She took a long breath, paused, then made a decision to continue. "The plutonium the scientists had developed is even safer to handle. It doesn't require thick lead shielding as did earlier nuclear materials. A small, relatively light, specially lined carrying case would protect anyone carrying a bomb made from the new plutonium from radiation poisoning."

"How does the plutonium become a bomb?"

"That's where the expertise starts," Tolstoy replied. "First the material has to be shaped into a perfect sphere— about the size of a tennis ball. In technical circles it is called a 'pit.' That takes a well-equipped nuclear laboratory. Most countries do not have such a facility, except for those who already have nuclear weapons or those who are actively trying to develop one."

"At least that rules out terrorist groups."

Tolstoy laughed cynically. "If you were a country backing terrorists, would you let them have the raw materials for manufacturing a bomb?"

Bolan understood. "What happens after the tennis ball is made?"

"To make the bomb reach critical mass and set off a chain reaction—you would call it nuclear fission—you have to make the pit implode on itself. That requires a tremendous bang from about eight hundred to one thousand pounds of explosives packed evenly around the sphere. The explosives have to go off at exactly the same time, which requires precise timing devices capable of releasing rapid bursts of electricity."

"We've had attempts made to steal high-energy capacitors from research firms in our country," the soldier replied. "As far as we know, no one has been successful. At least, not yet."

"We're talking about a miniaturized bomb with only twenty percent of the energy of the devices dropped on Hiroshima," Tolstoy added. "But still enough to cause the deaths of more than a hundred thousand innocent men, women and children in a city like Tel Aviv, Seoul, Moscow or even your Washington, D.C."

"You know your stuff about nuclear weapons," he commented with admiration.

"Much of it I learned in your country," she replied.

Bolan was curious. "Why did you come back to Russia after you graduated from Cal Tech? There was no shortage of jobs available in the United States for someone with your knowledge and experience."

The woman's reply was simple and direct. "Because I am a Russian. If men and women like me deserted Russia, who would be left? The malcontents? Those who would like to see people like Stalin back in power? Criminals like the mafia? Those who would rape Russia of its dignity and potential?" She shook her head. "I had no choice but to come back."

"I read an article that claimed that there were no heroes left in Russia," he commented. "The article was wrong. There are heroes. People like you, who are willing to fight to save their country."

The colonel's face reddened. "Thank you," she said softly.

"You're welcome."

She swallowed the rest of her wine and filled the glass again. Bolan sipped his beer and thought about what the woman had said. He weighed the options they had, then said, "At least we're going to have to make sure no psychopath gets to use their knowledge."

The Russian colonel sipped her wine in silence, then reluctantly nodded. "Agreed . . . as a last resort."

Tolstoy looked at her wristwatch. "But it is time to go home. We can continue this conversation tomorrow in my office."

OUTSIDE THE HOTEL the two occupants of a parked police car sat and waited.

Lieutenant Leonid Lubov sat beside the uniformed driver in the small car. He kept staring at the ornate entrance to the

Radisson Slavyanskaya Hotel for the appearance of Irina Tolstoy and the big American.

He would have to wait until they left central Moscow before he could make his move. The street was too crowded with tourists and cars to attempt to stop the pair.

The orders had been explicit. The American was to be killed, but it had to look as if he had tried to escape arrest and had shot at them. The orders had come from Major-General Donielev's aide, Colonel Federov.

Lubov had worked on the side for the former KGB colonel before the secret police had been dismantled, doing special jobs, such as shooting a political figure who had opposed the KGB, and a novelist who made it his business to tell the foreign press how terrible the Soviet Union had become had died in his sleep.

"You owe me," the colonel had reminded him. "Your promotions, your home, the money you have in a foreign bank account, your freedom, all came from my help."

"But murdering an American?" The police lieutenant looked frightened.

The colonel laughed. "It wouldn't be the first time you killed someone. But this time it is a criminal trying to get away from the police. If someone questions you, it was a mistake but an understandable one. You will be paid well as soon as you complete your mission.

"And you will be given enough money so that you and your family can emigrate to another country and start a new and better life if you are dismissed."

"The officer who will be driving..."

"I'll make sure he is also taken care of," Donielev promised.

"Where will I find the American?"

"When he was released from headquarters, he and the woman were going to the Radisson for a conference with some American official. Wait outside for them, follow them and find some place where it is less crowded. Perhaps on

Volgograder Street. They have to use the boulevard whether they go to the American's hotel or to the woman's apartment."

"How will I know he's the right American? Many of them stay at the hotel."

"One of my men works there as a taxi driver. He has been given a full description of the American. Watch for his signal."

"Perhaps I should have some backup," the lieutenant had added nervously. "Just in case he manages to get away."

"I've arranged for it," Federov replied. "But make it your business not to miss."

The police lieutenant had hung up the phone and stared at his desk for a minute. Life was getting too complicated in Russia. The things one had to do to put food on the table, he complained privately as he opened his desk drawer and took out the Tokarev automatic he kept there.

Pulling the drawer out farther, he had found tools, oil and a rag. Carefully he dismantled the handgun and began to clean it.

It was important that none of the rounds jammed because of some stray dirt in the barrel. After all, this American just might have a gun of his own.

BOLAN AND TOLSTOY PAUSED outside the hotel.

"You drank a few glasses of wine," he reminded her. "Are you sure you're okay to drive?"

She laughed. "You forget I am a Russian. I learned to drink before I learned to walk."

Tolstoy headed to where she'd parked her car, then stopped and turned. "Until tomorrow," she said, and unlocked her car door.

Neither of them saw the shabbily dressed cab driver pointing out Bolan to the occupants of the GAZ police car parked across the street.

Bolan turned and approached the parking attendant. Handing him the ticket Brognola had given him, Bolan waited. Within minutes he could hear the screeching of tires as a driver traveled the parking ramps at top speed.

When the garage attendant jammed on the brakes and stopped the car, Bolan looked at the ancient Russian-built Volga. The vehicle still bore the dents from dozens of encounters with other Moscow drivers, and he hoped the big Fed hadn't handed him a lemon.

A second man got out of the Volga. He was huge, with the build of someone who had been a prizefighter or a policeman. Brognola had said he was having the car guarded. The man nodded to Bolan and strolled out of the garage.

The soldier got behind the wheel and shut the door. As he started the engine, he could hear the power in the modified engine. Brognola hadn't exaggerated. Under the hood of the Russian car was the engine of an American hot rod.

Leaving the hotel garage, Bolan maneuvered through the street. Even at that late hour taxis and cars, blaring their horns in frustration, jammed the roadway, making it difficult to move.

Trucks and foot traffic from the Kiev Railway Station, right next door to the hotel, added to the confusion. Gypsies, who used the huge station as their temporary living quarters, kept dashing into the street, banging on windows and begging for handouts.

Finally Bolan worked his way out of the area and headed for the nearest main boulevard.

Unlike the area around the Kiev Railway Station, traffic on Volgograder Street was almost nonexistent. The broad road, which led to the southeastern outskirts of the city, was dimly lit. Armed drunks had used the tall streetlights as targets. Typically the authorities hadn't gotten around to replacing them.

Bolan glanced in the rearview mirror and saw a small Moscow police car moving toward him at high speed.

Someone in the vehicle suddenly turned on the rotating light atop the car.

For a moment Bolan wasn't sure whom they were chasing. Then he realized it was him.

He leaned forward and rammed the gas pedal to the floor. The small car responded immediately, picking up speed.

He glanced into the rearview mirror. The police car had to have been modified, too, he decided. It was still gaining on him.

A whining ricochet startled him. Through the rearview mirror he could see a uniformed cop leaning out of the passenger-side window, holding a late-model 5.45 mm AK-74 assault rifle against his cheekbone. The swerving of the cars caused the continuous spray of lead sizzlers from the Kalashnikov's 30-round magazine to travel far from their mark—him.

But Bolan knew that there was always the chance of a lucky shot. Normally he would haul out the Beretta he wore under his jacket and shoot back. But these were policemen. A deep-seated belief that they were soldiers on the same side prevented him from killing cops.

The Executioner decided to try to widen the odds without returning the fire. Twisting the steering wheel to the right, he almost ran the small car onto the sidewalk, then wrenched the wheel in the opposite direction.

As he had suspected, the driver of the police car was trying to imitate his actions. Both cars weaved across the wide road at high speed. Suddenly Bolan spun the wheel again and let the car run onto the sidewalk.

He glanced at the rearview mirror.

As he had suspected it would, the police vehicle followed him onto the sidewalk. Easing up on the gas pedal, he let the Volga slow. The cop car kept charging at top speed.

Just as the official car was about to hit him, Bolan did a "wheelie" and jammed down on the brakes.

The souped-up car made a 180-degree turn. Bolan lifted his foot off the brake and pressed the gas pedal to the floor again.

Behind him the police driver had lost control. Despite his efforts to turn the official car, the vehicle stopped hard against the trunk of a wide tree. Steam started to pour from the ruptured radiator.

The uniformed lieutenant grabbed the AK-74 from the wrecked car and cut loose again. Screaming lead tore into the rear of the Volga, and sooner or later one of the rounds was going to find a target—him.

Bolan stopped the car. Shoving the door open, he rolled out of the vehicle and onto the grass. He made a quick decision. They weren't interested in arresting him. They wanted him dead.

All the reservations he had about firing at cops were set aside for now. Survival came first. He would have to fight back if he wanted to stay alive.

The two uniformed men charged at him, both firing AK-74s from their hips like six shooters. The soldier hugged the ground, making himself as small a target as he could.

Waiting for them to come closer, he gripped the Beretta 93-R with both hands and focused it on the nearer of the two, the man who wore a lieutenant's uniform.

Several rounds shattered the rear window of the Volga. Others chewed the boulevard asphalt. Finally the Executioner decided he could wait no longer.

Switching to autofire, he unleashed a short burst of lead that almost tore the officer's head from his body. Blood streamed wildly from the ruptured arteries and covered the roadway as the skull and body tumbled to the ground.

The other uniformed man kept charging, emptying the 30-round magazine in Bolan's direction. The soldier had changed position before resuming the battle. Now hidden behind the Volga's trunk, the Executioner fired another burst that ruptured the attacker's chest. Shredded viscera pushed out of the suddenly yawning cavity in the gunman's torso before the man crumpled.

Somebody wanted Bolan out of the way badly.

The soldier knew that he wasn't home free yet. The police officers might have backup waiting to continue the attack.

He climbed into the battle-scarred Volga and drove away. Several hundred yards later his gut feeling proved correct.

An armored vehicle lumbered into the roadway from a side street. He recognized it as a BTR-40 APC, fitted with the Soviet version of the 7.62 mm M-72 AB-1 machine gun.

The gunner sitting behind the mounted weapon spun the turret and pointed the machine gun at Bolan's vehicle. A torrent of lead washed the area. Most of the shots flew wide of their target, but a few tore through the hood and chewed into the engine.

There was too much distance between the armored car and Bolan's vehicle for his shots to be effective. There was nothing left to do but run.

The soldier pushed the door open and jumped into the roadway, letting the Volga continue its movement forward. A quick side roll absorbed the impact with the asphalt. Pulling himself into a sitting position, the Executioner whipped out the Beretta and waited.

The darkness had masked his escape. The Volga kept rolling toward the armored vehicle, absorbing round after round of lead from the machine gun mounted on top of the BTR-40.

A second gunman popped up from inside the military vehicle, touching shoulders with the machine gunner. Bolan recognized the weapon jammed against the second man's shoulder—a 40 mm BG-15 grenade launcher mounted beneath an AK-74 assault rifle. There were only two types of grenades the Russian weapon fired: the 7P-17, an impact, high-explosive fragmentation grenade, or the more deadly

VOG-25, a bouncing grenade with a delay element in the nose.

Bolan hoped it was the former. There was less chance of injury from ricochets.

The grenade smashed through the front windshield of the Volga and tore the interior into shreds. Burning chunks of metal flew in every direction, narrowly missing Bolan.

He lifted his head and saw the gunman loading a second grenade into the launcher.

Time to get out of there, he told himself, scrambling to his feet. Using the darkened sidewalk for cover, he darted between a pair of decrepit apartment buildings and down an alley. All the lights in the buildings were extinguished. Bolan suspected the tenants were hiding on the floors of their apartments and would stay there until the shooting stopped.

There was a connecting alley at the rear. Running along the sides of the buildings, he masked his movements in the shadows of the structures. He moved quickly to where the alley emptied into a side street. Cautiously he peered around the corner.

He could hear the loud crackling sounds of the Volga exploding, and the shouts of the police as they converged on it.

They'd be too busy looking for bodies in the wreckage to search the area for him. At least he hoped so.

He looked around for transportation.

An ancient Chaika was parked at the curb. It was slow and noisy, but it would serve his immediate needs. He scanned for onlookers, then used his jacket to soften the sound of breaking the glass in the driver's door.

Bolan reached in to release the door latch, then opened the door and slid behind the wheel. He knew that whoever owned the aged vehicle had probably invested at least a year's wages to buy it.

There was a glove box mounted beneath the dashboard, and he opened it. An official-looking document had the name, address and telephone of the owner. He'd leave money in the compartment and call the owner to tell him where to find his car when he was done with it.

The soldier hot-wired the ignition, and the engine started immediately. As he pulled away from the curb, Bolan suspected his hotel was probably being watched. Irina Tolstoy's home was a possibility, but he didn't have her address. And he wasn't sure if he completely trusted her yet. Then he remembered the one person he could trust.

Smiling grimly, he decided Hal Brognola was going to have a roommate for the night.

8

"What do you mean there wasn't a body? There had to be at least one body in the wreckage," the ex-KGB general roared into the telephone.

"There were two bodies, General. But they were those of the police officers I hired to kill the American," Federov reported.

"Go to the hotel where he is staying. Take as many men as you need and kill him there, if necessary!"

Federov was an oasis of calm. "I took four of my best men and went there. He hasn't been back all evening."

"Find him," Donielev ordered.

"Where would you suggest we start, General?"

The ex-KGB division head became silent as he thought about possible hideouts. Then he remembered that Lena Kurilov had told him that the American would be at the old KGB headquarters the following morning.

He told Federov.

"We will get him on his way out," the former colonel promised, and hung up.

Donielev was pleased. Federov was a solid man. He wouldn't dare to miss twice.

Michael Belasko was spending his last night on earth. The general hoped he was enjoying it.

MACK BOLAN ENTERED the yellow-colored six-level building on what was once called Dzerzhinsky Square but had been renamed Lubyankaya Place since the disbanding of the KGB.

The KGB hadn't been just an intelligence agency: it had been a terrifying, repressive, secret-police monolith that controlled the lives of ordinary Soviet citizens and most of the country's leaders, and fought in the trenches of the cold war as well. When the USSR broke up in late 1991, so did the KGB, though some said that the vast organization had simply metastasized.

Moscow's Intelligence service might have changed its name, but based on Bolan's experience with the men and women who had run the organization, it probably hadn't changed its method of operation.

That was certainly true of the overseas espionage organization, the Foreign Intelligence Service—or SVR—which reported directly to the Russian president. It was the first segment of the old KGB to open for business on its own in October 1991. The SVR took over most of the spies and analysts from the parent organization.

Another piece of the KGB was turned into the Federal Agency for Government Communications and Information, which was the Russian equivalent of the U.S. National Security Agency. An additional eight thousand troops joined the Presidential Guard, similar to the American Secret Service. Domestic investigations went to the Russian FBI equivalent, the FSK, which had a staff of seventy-five thousand and was in charge of internal security.

The Russians Bolan had listened to were poor-mouthing the SVR, claiming that it had cut its staff forty percent over the past three years—without giving any actual numbers—and had closed thirty overseas stations.

While the SVR may have shrunk, Bolan knew it was still active and highly professional. He had watched as Russian spies burrowed for U.S. secrets long after the Soviet Union disintegrated.

Now the building he was about to enter had become the headquarters for the newly formed SVR. Obviously representatives of other agencies maintained some presence there, such as Irina Tolstoy.

Wearing the sports jacket and slacks he had worn on the flight, Bolan stopped at the long counter that barred visitors from the elevators behind it.

"Who do you wish to see?" The icy words came from the thin-lipped woman behind the counter.

"Colonel Irina Tolstoy," the soldier said as he looked around the lobby.

The only way to the elevators was past an electronic surveillance gate. He was glad he had decided to leave the Beretta and the combat knife in Brognola's hotel suite. The rest of his arsenal was hidden in his own hotel room.

The woman consulted a large loose-leaf notebook, then lifted a phone and dialed a number. She whispered into the phone before nodding and replacing the handset.

"Someone will come and get you," she said without the hint of a smile.

Bolan turned and looked out of the windows of the lobby. Dzerzhinsky Square had changed dramatically. The once forbidding statue of the founder of the secret police, Felix Dzerzhinsky, had vanished from its huge pedestal. Boxes of flowers bloomed where once only concrete squares had stood.

A young woman in the uniform of a lieutenant approached him.

"Mr. Belasko?" Lena Kurilov said.

"Yes," he replied, smiling as he turned and recognized Tolstoy's aide.

"The colonel is ready to see you."

He followed the young woman through the security checkpoint and into an elevator.

IRINA TOLSTOY LOOKED UP from the stack of papers she'd been studying and saw the Executioner standing in her doorway. Smiling, she took off her thin, fashionable glasses and pushed the papers to one side of her desk.

"Come in, Mr. Belasko. Have a seat."

She turned to the young lieutenant. "I'll have black tea, Lena."

Then Tolstoy asked Bolan, "Something to drink?"

"The same," he said.

The lieutenant vanished and closed the door behind her.

The soldier looked around the room. It had the same dingy look that government offices in Washington, D.C., had. The only difference was the woman behind the desk. Even in the ill-fitting uniform she wore, Irina Tolstoy managed to look attractive.

"I thought you were with the Ministry of Atomic Energy," Bolan commented.

"I am. But when the KGB disbanded, I asked my minister if I could maintain my office here where I had spent so many years of my life."

Bolan remembered. According to Brognola's file, when the then-major Tolstoy went to the United States she was with the section of the KGB that dealt with nuclear matters. He wondered if she was still connected with the SVR.

As if she had read his mind, the colonel commented, "No, Mr. Belasko, I am not with the SVR in any capacity. My sole interest in you is to get whatever help you can give us in finding the scientists and their stolen containers."

"I wondered," Bolan commented, and told her what had happened the previous night.

"I'd have the police officers interrogated," Tolstoy replied, "if they weren't dead. The attack could have been a response to your killing the gangsters in the park."

"Are you saying the men I shot weren't cops?"

"Anybody can be hired for enough money," Tolstoy replied.

"What about the pair in the BTR?"

"Weapons and military vehicles are stolen daily by the mafia. Usually they just resell them out of the country. In your case they may have decided you were an important enough target to test them on first."

The lieutenant returned with a tray that held two cups, a bowl of sugar and a small, steaming samovar. She set the tray on a corner of the desk and left again.

As she poured tea into the cups, Tolstoy continued to talk. "I suppose we'll never know if last night was a gang response. And in a way, what happened was probably for the best. At least we know that somebody wants to kill Michael Belasko."

As USUAL there was a long line waiting to get into the American embassy. The sidewalk was nearly blocked by the long queue of visa applicants waiting to get permission to visit the United States.

The tall, patrician-looking man ran a hand through his long, graying hair. Smoothing the conservatively cut jacket of his suit, the fifty-five-year-old former CIA official stopped and stared at the strange assortment of people in the line.

Young men and women mingled with the elderly, all wanting to escape the harsh reality of life in Russia. In line with them were the new breed of businessmen, each wanting a chance to try his luck at acquiring goods in the United States and shipping their acquisitions back to Moscow, where they could resell them at a five hundred percent profit, after all expenses. Stand-ins, usually low-level members of one of the local mafia gangs, forced their way into the line, glaring at anyone who tried to challenge them. The wait sometimes took half a day, so the person who was paying to wait wouldn't be called to take their place in the long line until they were ready to move into the embassy building.

Max Haverford was disgusted by the spectacle. America had finally succumbed to the weaklings who currently ran the government. Anyone could get a visa—at least anyone who didn't have a criminal record.

Even that could be handled for a fee.

When he was running the Soviet desk at the Central Intelligence Agency, he would lecture the people in the field to protect their sources from being identified as criminals or former members of the KGB.

That was how Yuri Donielev and he had met.

The former KGB general had sent a message about sensitive information he was willing to turn over to the CIA in exchange for a passport. After studying the files on him, the new Agency director had turned down Donielev's offer.

Instead, Haverford was sent to Russia to see what other kind of deal could be negotiated for the secret KGB files.

Donielev withdrew his offer to the American government and, instead, made one to the CIA representative.

Haverford could remember the conversation over a spectacular dinner at the elegant LeRomanoff restaurant on the second floor of the Baltschug Hotel. The powerfully built ex-KGB general had provided the companions, two young, beautiful women with ready smiles and bodies that would have made an American movie starlet proud.

"Perhaps I will stay in Russia, after all," Donielev announced. "There are fortunes to be made right here. Especially in Moscow. There are many gangs, but not one of them has a real leader. Not a leader like me.

"However, I will need a partner. Someone with the freedom to travel and to negotiate deals with groups outside of Russia."

"By groups you mean foreign governments?"

"Exactly. Foreign governments." He leaned over and pounded Haverford on the shoulder. "You do understand, don't you?"

Haverford had spent too many years protecting his rear to agree to anything without a fuller explanation.

"What kind of deals did you have in mind?"

The general leaned across the table and spoke softly into the American's ear. "Many things. Military arms. Surplus vehicles. Gold mined in the Asian republics. Drugs. Thousands of metric tons of drugs grow right here in Russia and the other Soviet republics. And information. All kinds of information. I have file cabinets filled with the kind of information foreign governments would pay handsomely to have. Especially information on where our dismantled missiles are stored and how to get them."

Haverford was impressed. "You'd sell them to a foreign government?"

"For enough money, yes. You could be a partner on these foreign deals. We would share equally what remained after I took care of those who helped us."

Haverford was about to turn down the offer, then he thought of the pension he would be receiving. It was barely enough to let him survive. And retirement was coming fast. A clean sweep of the hard-liners, like himself, had been rumored for months.

He'd have to watch Donielev carefully. But he, not the Russian, had the contacts with foreign Intelligence services.

"I was planning to open a consulting firm when I retired," he said, throwing out bait.

"And I will be one of your first clients," Donielev promised.

Haverford lifted the glass of wine sitting on the table in front of him.

"To our mutual success," he said, and waited for Donielev to raise his glass.

AS THE FORMER CIA official pushed his way through the crowds, he reflected on the size of his bank account in Bahrain. The tiny Arab state was the center of finance in the Middle East, and a safe place to hide his profits from the nosy agents of the IRS.

More than five million dollars had been transferred to his account in the three years since he'd retired from the Agency and started his firm.

The money he received from clients wasn't all profits, he reminded himself as he entered the embassy. The previous week ten thousand dollars had been moved into a Caribbean bank account controlled by an Agency staff member in the Moscow embassy. The money was Haverford's way of thanking the young man for tipping him to the visit by American law enforcement officials to discuss the mafia problem in the Russian capital.

The source's information had been right on target, even if the point man Donielev's men tried to kill had killed them instead.

Retrieving the Agency pass he still carried and showing it to the Marine sergeant on guard outside the embassy building gained him immediate entrance. A ride to the third floor on the fast, quiet elevator, and a short walk to a small office near the end of the main corridor brought him to Jason Lassiter.

The shirtsleeved CIA representative looked up from the stack of papers in front of him and saw Haverford walk into the office and close the door behind him.

Surprised, he pointed to the empty chair on the opposite side of the small wooden desk. "What's the occasion?"

Haverford eased into the chair. "Have you read the local papers lately?"

"Every day. Why?"

"Six men were killed in Ismailovsky Park yesterday. The police arrested an American, who they claimed killed the men, then released him because they claimed the six were members of a local gang."

Lassiter held up a copy of the local English-language daily. "I read it. The Moscow police also found the partially destroyed body of an elderly man, whom they haven't been able to identify yet. The dead men were in the middle of burying him when the American stopped them. Why are you interested?"

Haverford pointed to the small radio sitting on Lassiter's credenza. The CIA representative understood and turned it on, tuning in a loud rock-and-roll station.

"I'm not interested. Not in the dead men," the ex-CIA section chief said, trying to make himself heard over the musical noise. "It's the American who intrigues me. Not many men can kill six men by himself." He forced a smile. "What do you know about him?"

"Not much, except for his name." He searched the paper-laden desk and found a photocopied sheet of paper. "His name is Michael Belasko, and he's part of the law enforcement delegation from the United States that has come to advise the Russians on how to deal with the mafia problem here."

He dropped the page on the desk. "That's all they wrote as far as yours truly is concerned."

Haverford leaned forward. "What else do you know about him? Height? Weight? Background? Who'd he work for before he came here?"

"No can do. He must be pretty high up the food chain. We got a 'hands-off' memo about Belasko. If he asks for help, we're supposed to give it to him. But, otherwise, we keep out of his way." He hesitated, then lowered his voice. "I'll tell you this much. There's more to this Michael Belasko than is in a file. Some of the old-timers around here say his way of working—you know, alone and without supervision—reminds them of somebody else. But that guy is supposed to be dead, which is probably a blessing for everybody else."

"Who was that somebody else?"

"I don't know if you Langley types had ever run into him. His name was Mack Bolan, and he was one mean son of a bitch, according to the stories I've heard."

It was time Donielev and he talked about this Belasko, and tried to come up with a plan to kill him, Haverford thought.

If Belasko was Bolan, they'd kill two threats with one death. If he wasn't, they'd be getting rid of a nuisance.

Either way they couldn't lose, Haverford decided.

9

His business concluded, Mack Bolan left the former KGB headquarters.

He stopped to look at the relaxed expressions on the faces of passersby before he headed for the side street where he'd parked the replacement car the embassy had provided. He had selected another retooled Volga. It was small and inconspicuous, and if the same mechanic had worked on the engine, the vehicle had a lot of horses under its hood.

In every direction Bolan saw symbols of the nouveau riche of Russia: jewels around the neck of an attractive, well-dressed woman who was window-shopping; custom-tailored suits on two aggressive-looking businessmen almost trotting past him as they rushed to an appointment; a pair of Irish wolfhounds straining against their leashes as a uniformed driver struggled to keep them in tow.

A silver Mercedes-Benz 500 SL sports car with its top down drove past him and stopped at the curb. Bolan knew the vehicle sold for more than a quarter-million American dollars in Russia.

He couldn't see the face of the man behind the wheel. An older man, Bolan decided, and bald. He knew the driver could only be one of three things: a black marketer, one of the new breed Russian wheeler-dealers or the head of one of the mafia gangs.

A black-haired young woman leaned over, kissed the man on the lips, then opened the car door and got out.

Bolan recognized Lieutenant Kurilov, Colonel Tolstoy's aide.

As the imported car sped away, she studied the watch on her wrist, then turned and saw Bolan. Kurilov seemed flustered, then braced herself and walked to him.

"Mr. Belasko, are you finished with your meeting?"

Bolan nodded.

"I should hurry. The colonel will need my services."

She pulled back the sleeve of her jacket and glanced at her wristwatch. "I've been gone only fifteen minutes," she added defensively, then turned and rushed into the building.

There was something about her that bothered him. Then he realized it was her watch. She wore a Rolex, surrounded by small diamonds.

How did someone afford that kind of watch on a lieutenant's salary?

Bolan wondered if he'd found the source of the leaks.

He'd have to ask Irina Tolstoy to tell him more about Kurilov. And who was this boyfriend of hers?

AT THE SUBURBAN DACHA, Donielev looked at his visitor. The tall, well-dressed American eased himself into a soft chair and lit a cuban cigar.

The former KGB general kept staring at the silent telephone.

"Something wrong?" Haverford asked.

"No," Donielev said quickly. "I'm just expecting a call from Federov."

Haverford wanted the Russian to stay with the subject that had brought him out to the suburban compound on a busy working day.

"Why does Mike Belasko want to kill you?"

"I don't know."

"I tried to find out what he's really doing here from my embassy contacts," Haverford said, "but they're as much in the dark as you."

Then he changed the subject. "Have you heard from the government?"

"Yes. They've agreed to pay the ransom. Tonight in Sokolniki Park, as our letter demanded."

"Good. So have the Iranians."

"How do we do this?"

"I've arranged for a plane to fly me to the Azerbaijan Republic tomorrow. I have a date to meet the Iranian representative in Baku."

As a native of that part of the Caucasus Mountains, which touched Azerbaijan, Donielev had been to Baku many times, both as a boy and later as a member of the counterintelligence division.

When he was promoted to general of the Second Directorate, he had recruited some of his most loyal aides in Baku. Many had been with him for more than ten years. Most had followed when he was forced to retire from the Committee for State Security by the Russian traitors who had taken over the government. Except for those who had been killed in battles with other mafia groups who objected to his invasion of what they had considered their exclusive businesses, the others were still with him.

Haverford had made a good choice in selecting Baku as the exchange point. The capital of the former Soviet republic sat on the edge of the Caspian Sea and faced Iran. Even though both were predominantly Muslim countries, the Azeris distrusted their neighbors and the fundamentalist religious revolution they were trying to impose on the nations around them.

The American got up from the living room easy chair. "Time I was getting back to my office," he said, then walked to the door. He turned and said, "What I don't understand is why you are personally going to oversee the paying of the ransom. It could be dangerous."

"I have made plans to counter any attempts to take us into custody," the former general assured him.

"Why can't Federov pick up the money and bring it here?"

Donielev stared at the American with an expression of disbelief. "I trust no one with my money," he replied bluntly.

Haverford knew the Russian's distrust extended to him, as well as his own men. "Fine."

"I have only one concern. The men I cannot take with me. The ones we recruited here." He paused. "What to do about them?"

The American shrugged. "Once you have the money, does it really matter what happens to them?"

"They could be forced to talk," Donielev warned.

"Not if they are found dead."

Donielev stared at Haverford coldly, then a sly smile began to play at the corners of his mouth. "I like the way you are thinking," he commented.

"We each have our work cut out for us," the American said.

"When will you pick up the professors and their nuclear samples?"

"In the morning. I'll drive them to the airport myself. See you in Baku," Haverford said.

"I have a better idea. Meet me in Sokolniki Park tonight. We can spend the night here, celebrating. I'll have my men drive you to the airport in the morning."

Haverford knew the Russian well enough to understand he had just been given an order.

"I'll be there an hour before the scheduled meeting. Any idea who will delivering the money?"

"Some bureaucratic employees, I suppose."

The American started to leave the living room.

Donielev stopped him. "What about this man Belasko?"

"Kill him before he can get to you."

"But how?" Donielev seemed perplexed.

Haverford smiled. "Perhaps your girlfriend could bring him to you."

The Russian weighed the suggestion, then made a decision. "Yes. And maybe it is time to get a new girlfriend."

BOLAN HAD PARKED the Volga around the corner from the entrance to the KGB building. As he approached the vehicle, his combat senses flared, warning him that danger was nearby.

He stopped at the window of an antique store that catered to foreign visitors and looked at the reflections in the glass.

Two men stood near the car, trying hard not to look at him. The clothes they wore seemed simple, and the metallic-thread ties they wore were typical neck wear for Russian men. But the dead expression on their faces, and the coldness of their eyes, were plain giveaways that these were street soldiers, not ordinary businessmen.

Bolan tapped the side of his jacket, then remembered he had left his guns under the seat of his car.

The one thing he knew for sure was that the bulges in the jackets of the two men were made by weapons—probably Uzi or Skorpion submachine guns from their shape and length.

He saw another possible problem making a turn onto the crowded side street, a gray BMW.

The volume of cars trying to move on the narrow street slowed them enough that he could look inside.

Five men sat inside the luxury vehicle, all of them with the facial expressions of hardmen. Except for one. He wore a crew cut and sat with the rigid dignity of a military officer.

But all of them stared in his direction.

There were too many innocents on the street to start a battle, even if he had weapons. He had to select a less crowded site for the fight he sensed was coming.

The Volga was parked at the curb ten yards away.

Thinking fast, he formulated a plan. Turning from the shop window, Bolan started to walk slowly at an angle toward the Volga. As he neared the two hardmen, he spun and wrapped a muscular forearm around the neck of the closer one.

The sudden action stunned both men. Bolan wasn't sure what reaction his movement had gotten from the occupants of the large BMW, but he'd worry about them later.

Yanking open the jacket of the man he held in a throat lock, he turned up the autoloader hanging from a shoulder rig and pointed it at the second hardman.

There was no time to worry about releasing a safety. Besides, he was certain the weapon was ready to be fired immediately when the right opportunity arrived.

Checking for bystanders and aiming carefully, the Executioner drilled the chest and stomach of the hardman standing there.

Then, letting go of the submachine gun, he twisted the neck of his adversary he held. A loud cracking sound echoed in the immediate vicinity as the now-dead gunner slumped forward.

Bolan tore the 9 mm Skorpion subgun from the body, then retrieved the weapon the other hardman had carried.

There was no time to search for additional clips. He would have to make do with what he had.

Ignoring the horrified expressions on the faces of passersby, he shoved the key into the Volga's lock, twisted it and jerked the door open. Jumping in, he shoved the key into the ignition, turned it, and floored the gas pedal.

In the rearview mirror he could see the gray BMW trying to get around the vehicles that had come between it and the small Volga. It was only a matter of time before the men in the chase car would get tired of playing games and start shooting at him.

He was certain they had no qualms about killing innocent people, as long as they killed him, as well. What he wasn't certain of was why they wanted him dead.

Was it revenge for the six dead thugs, or something more ominous?

The first break came when he raced through an intersection just ahead of a large truck. He could hear the sounds of gunfire behind him. Checking in the rearview mirror, Bolan saw one of the BMW's passengers jump out of the vehicle and, pointing a gun at the truck driver, force him to back up.

The Executioner made a series of tight turns in and out of the narrow streets until he finally reached a broad boulevard and turned into it.

He checked the mirror. The German-made luxury car was charging down the broad boulevard in hot pursuit. The eight cylinders under its hood provided the power it needed to catch up with Bolan. Even retooled, the small, 4-cylinder Volga was no match for the bigger vehicle.

The Executioner picked up one of the Skorpion SMGs from the seat next to him, leaned out of the open window and fired back at the BMW. The tires on the pursuing vehicle were made of thick rubber. But the soldier knew that no tire was totally bulletproof.

Suddenly the BMW's right front tire exploded. The vehicle swerved wildly to the right and, before the driver could bring the car out of the spin, ran into a parked truck. It spun from the impact, then jumped into the air nose first, landed on its back and burst into flames.

Bolan stopped the car, grabbed the second Skorpion SMG and moved cautiously to the crash site.

The men who had intended to kill him had been thrown clear of the wreck. The one with the crew cut looked vaguely familiar.

No one had survived the crash.

10

The phone rang in Hal Brognola's hotel suite.

Bolan heard it in the bathroom, where he was busy using tweezers to remove slivers of glass from his face and hands. The head Fed, before he left to meet with the others from the United States, had offered to call a doctor from the embassy, but Bolan had rejected the idea.

"The fewer who know where I am, the better my chances of staying alive."

The soldier was using the suite while Brognola had breakfast with the Americans who would be participating in the law-enforcement conference. It was safer than going back to his own hotel.

He let the phone ring again, then finally picked it up. Before he could say anything, the female voice on the other end spoke. "This is Colonel Tolstoy. If you can reach Mr. Belasko, please tell him to call me. It is urgent."

"I'm here, Irina. What's up?"

There was the sound of relief over the telephone line.

"I heard about the battle around the corner from my building. When I got there, bystanders described you as the killer who had gotten away."

"A little inaccurate," Bolan replied, then told her what had really happened, including the battle on the boulevard.

"According to my contacts, the police are attributing that explosion to a faulty gasoline tank."

"Lucky for me, it was their aim that was faulty."

"You don't know just how lucky you were. One of the dead men found near the wreckage was Vasily Federov, a former KGB colonel and personal aide to Major-General Yuri Donielev. An expert shot."

She paused, then asked, "Are you all right?"

"Scratches here and there," he assured her. "Not enough damage to keep me from going after Donielev."

"I may be able to help you. I spent the past hour calling everywhere I could think of to find you. I tried your hotel, but there was no answer in your room. And they connected me with somebody who demanded I identify myself. So I hung up and took a chance on calling Mr. Brognola."

"Somebody is looking for you," she went on. "A number of men who have some association with Donielev have been calling their contacts and asking questions about you."

"What kind of questions?"

"Why you are here. Do you have any connection to—and I quote one of them—'the late Mack Bolan.'" She sounded worried. "Word about Federov's death has them edgy."

"Good."

"Not good. These are vermin. Like any rats they are most dangerous when they believe they are cornered."

"They'll find out tonight just how cornered they are," Bolan reminded her, "when we deliver the ransom."

"I told you it was my responsibility."

He used the simplest argument, rather than wasting a lot of time in useless discussion. "It's my country's money you're using."

Tolstoy remained silent a moment, then asked, "What if the people who claimed they have the two scientists decide not to show up?"

"We go looking for them," Bolan replied.

"Perhaps I know where at least some of them are," Tolstoy said. "I still have some contacts within the FSK and with the Moscow police. There is a warehouse—supposedly abandoned. But for the past few months a large number of suspicious-looking men have been going in and out of the building. I checked with the city. The warehouse is owned by a Russian company that is owned by Yuri Donielev."

"It sounds like that's his headquarters."

"None of the neighbors can identify him as one of the men entering the building. But they did identify two men from photographs, who have been in and out many times recently. Vasily Federov and Maxim Legulin. Federov was a colonel in the KGB. Legulin was a major. Federov headed up the wet assignments for the Second Directorate, and Legulin was his chief field operative. Between the two of them, and the team they led, a great number of people—many of them innocent of any crimes—were murdered."

The soldier knew that though the KGB may have vanished, many of the violent men and women who had worked for the organization were still living in and around Moscow. Many, like the dead KGB colonel, had just moved their skills to the mafia.

"And Donielev's men would probably know if the two nuclear experts were still in Moscow. And where they were being held," Tolstoy said. "It's worth checking out."

Bolan agreed.

"I'll pick you up in a half hour outside the hotel," she said, and hung up.

TOLSTOY SAT behind the wheel of an ancient Chaika parked at the curb. The doorman of the luxury hotel kept staring at the battered vehicle in disdain, obviously wishing the car wouldn't insult the reputation of the Radisson Slavyanskaya with its presence.

Mack Bolan came out through the large glass doors, dressed in casual clothes and carrying a long canvas bag. Ignoring the doorman's question if he could get him a cab, the soldier walked toward the Chaika.

The colonel motioned him to the driver's door and slid over. Bolan got behind the wheel.

"We are going to 30 Bolshaya Gruzinskaya Street in the Krasno-Presnensky District. It is not many miles from here," she said.

He looked at her. She had changed from the stern uniform she seemed to always wear. She now wore jeans, a turtleneck pullover and a worn leather jacket.

"I have to make a stop at my hotel," Bolan told her.

"There may be men waiting there."

"I can handle them. Then I'll drop you off at your office."

"I am going with you," she said firmly.

Bolan listened to the protesting engine of the small car. The Chaika was at least twenty-five years old. It had obviously survived a great number of encounters with other vehicles in its lifetime.

"We'll never make it there in this."

"Until he died, my father treated this car as one of his children." The redheaded woman ran a hand across the dashboard, caressing it. She looked at Bolan. "Usually I drive a government vehicle, but none was available when I called to requisition one."

She focused on the roadway. A surplus military vehicle was parked near the corner of a side street.

"Turn here," she ordered, "and stop next to the army command car."

A small, unoccupied UAZ-460 sat against the curb.

Bolan knew the vehicle. He had run into its clones in many of the places he had faced the Soviets and their allies. Like the American jeep, which had been its inspiration, the UAZ was a solidly built vehicle—a tough, reliable transport capable of speeds of up to sixty miles per hour. Like much of the military equipment in the Russian arsenals, thieves were stealing and selling the two-seaters for hard currency.

"A solid vehicle," she said in a low voice. "It will get us there."

Bolan nodded his agreement.

He pulled the Chaika in front of the Russian jeep and parked. While Tolstoy waited, the soldier checked to make sure no one was peering out of any of the apartment windows, then jimmied the driver's door open and got behind the wheel.

It took less than a minute to cross the right wires. Tolstoy hesitated for a moment, then opened the passenger door and got in.

She started to say something, but Bolan interrupted her.

"I'll call the owner and tell him where I left his car," he said as they started down the street.

DONIELEV FOUND TIME to chat with the two scientists. Both showed signs of fear.

One of them, Professor Davidov, asked, "When will the money be collected?"

"Soon," the mafia leader promised, forcing a smile on his face. "You may have to travel south for a few days to make the kidnapping seem legitimate."

Professor Sartov looked concerned. "To where, Yuri?"

"A small villa outside of Baku," Donielev replied, calmly. "While the Muscovites freeze up here, you will be sitting in the warm sun, getting a preview of what your life will be—after you get your share of the ransom money."

Sartov shook his head in regret. "If only Aleksandr hadn't changed his mind." He smiled at the ex-KGB official. "Have you heard anything about him?"

"Not much. Only that the ministry believed his story about being kidnapped and escaping. He sent a message to both of you that he thinks about you every day."

Sartov lifted a glass of vodka. "To Aleksandr Polsky. May we three be together again soon," he toasted.

The former KGB general smiled and joined in the toast, then apologized for having to get back to business.

He had a call to make to an old friend and former mentor, General Arkady Khreshchatik, the man who had instructed him on how to run a KGB directorate.

He hadn't seen his mentor since the retirement dinner both attended back in 1992. But he could still picture the man: tall, with the build of a prizefighter and long gray hair. His broad nose flared whenever he became angry. He was always impeccably dressed, waving the tobacco-stained cigarette holder as if it were a conductor's baton whenever he spoke.

Donielev was sure Khreshchatik would help him get rid of the American.

Closing the door behind him, he moved behind the antique desk in his office, opened his desk drawer and checked his personal phone book. Khreshchatik's unlisted number was in it.

The general answered the phone himself.

The former Second Directorate chief quickly exchanged pleasantries, then begged his former mentor to help him eliminate the American before he murdered every member of the mafia gangs in Russia.

"Calm yourself. I've been meaning to get together with you for some time now. Come to this address in two hours," Khreshchatik ordered. "It is a restaurant, but come alone. No bodyguards or weapons. We can talk there."

DONIELEV PARKED his sports car on a side street in the posh Lenin Hills district. Row after row of tall apartment buildings lined the broad streets. Built in the last days of the Soviet Union for the powerful and the rich, this was where the top politicians, businessmen and black marketers kept apartments.

Walking to the address his former chief had given him, Leninsky Prospekt 44, Donielev was astounded by the absence of noise. Central Moscow was constantly ringing with the sounds of cars, trucks, gunshots, people and loud music. Even the outskirts of the city where he lived had its own sounds: birds, the whine of jets overhead, the distant noises of farm machinery. But there was no sound here. It was as if he had entered a cemetery rather than an area where people lived.

He looked around for a restaurant sign but saw none.

There was a doorman in front of one of the buildings, and he approached the former KGB official. "General Donielev?"

He nodded, puzzled how the uniformed man knew his name.

"Follow me."

The man opened the front door of one of the numerous apartment buildings and pointed to a hallway. "It's at the end of the corridor."

Suspicious that this was a setup, Donielev moved cautiously along the empty hallway until he reached a glass door at its end.

He pushed it open. Stunned, he discovered he was in a restaurant, candlelit and decorated with statues of growling lions, armored knights and velvet-wrapped pillars.

A maître d' in a tuxedo joined him. "This way, General. Your party is waiting for you."

General Khreshchatik stood and greeted him with a hug and kiss on the cheek when he reached the large round table in the corner of the room. Donielev studied the man. He hadn't changed much from the last time they were together.

He looked at the faces of the other four men his former mentor had invited to lunch and recognized them. Each had been head of a KGB directorate, or second-in-command, until the agency had been shut down. Now each headed up one of the larger mafia gangs in Russia's capital.

Before the former KGB general could worry why the general had asked the four to join them, they greeted him warmly.

Khreshchatik pointed to an empty chair next to him. "Sit here, Yuri."

When Donielev complied, he said, "Now tell me what is going on."

Donielev decided to skip references to the kidnapping. Instead he discussed the continued murder of his men by an American.

"I believe this Michael Belasko is really the man we used to called the Executioner, the one who invaded a meeting of all the directorates and murdered so many fine men."

The elderly general next to him nodded. "I remember the incident. Fortunately I was out of the country at the time. And he came all the way from America to kill a former KGB general? You must be very important, Yuri."

"I don't know why he wants me dead," the ex-KGB official replied.

"Perhaps we do," his former mentor commented, and looked around to the others at the table nodding.

"Tell me," Donielev said humbly.

"You must have something he wants. Something he believes is his, not yours." He smiled at the nervous mafia chief. "That is also the reason we are here, Yuri. You have taken something each of us believes is his." His voice became harsh. "We want it back, Yuri."

Donielev looked stunned. He didn't know what the general meant.

"From me, you have tried to take over the trading of contraband goods," the elderly general said coldly. "I spent years building it, and now you dare intrude on what I've built."

"And from me, the prostitution trade," the former KGB official across the table growled.

"You are trying to gain control of the distribution and sale of narcotics," snapped a short, thin man who had headed the Fourth Directorate of the KGB.

The bitterness was painted across the man's face.

"The Azeris have always controlled the narcotics trade. We helped the farmers in the various republics to grow the best drugs by providing them with the finest seeds. We supplied the trucks and the men to process the narcotics. And we spent millions of rubles establishing a distribution network around the world. Now you come along and want to profit from the fruits of our hard work," he snarled.

"I have always controlled the protection business," a fourth man at the table snapped. "You offer protection for half the price I have charged."

"The others have always come to me when they needed someone eliminated," the former head of Directorate Z, the KGB division that eliminated dissidents, complained. "Now they don't know who to hire."

"Gentlemen, gentlemen," Khreshchatik said, trying to calm them, "we are all former comrades—friends—at this table."

He turned to Donielev. "That includes you, Yuri. Which is why you are not dead."

The elderly general looked at the others. "Am I not right?" Reluctantly they nodded.

"As of right now, you are out of business. We give you three days to put your affairs in order and leave Moscow. After that . . ." He left the sentence unfinished.

"If you don't believe us," Khreshchatik added, "check the warehouse where you store your contraband military equipment. You will find it empty and the men who guarded it dead."

Donielev felt the air rushing from his lungs. This was the last thing he had expected to happen.

His former mentor picked up a menu and studied it. "The food here is excellent, Yuri. I urge you to try the Staromoskovsky soup. It is made from a mushroom bouillon and is full of tender pieces of chicken and pork. Then you must taste the Zharkoye. You have never had a veal stew as delicious." He smiled at his former student. "But first we order vodka and drink to one another's continued good health."

Donielev was grateful the room was relatively dark so that none of the others could see how chalk white his face had become.

It was ironic. He had wished that there were a council such as this to which he could bring his troubles. Now it was here, and they were telling him he was the problem.

Suddenly, collecting the ransom from the Russian government had become essential. Added to the money he would get from the Iranians and the funds he had already deposited in foreign banks, he would be able to live well.

But not in Moscow.

Pushing his chair out, he stood. The waiter had placed a tall glass of vodka in front of him. He lifted it.

"To all of us," he toasted. "May we live long."

As the others lifted their glasses to join in the toast, Donielev wondered how long it would take for him to gather enough men to return and kill the men at the table.

Including Khreshchatik.

11

Bolan got behind the wheel and let Irina Tolstoy direct him to Bolshaya Gruzinskaya Street.

When they got there, he slowed down so he could study the outside, sensing that the supposedly deserted building was a setup. He aimed for a remote section of the high wall that encircled the warehouse and parked against it, then rechecked the magazine of the Beretta 93-R and the silenced Skorpion SMG he had taken from the dead mafia hit man.

He wore a canvas belt around his waist, and suspended from it was a trio of M-67 delay fragmentation grenades. The razor-sharp Applegate-Fairbairn combat knife lay snug in a thin sheath strapped to his right leg.

Bolan led the way from the military transport toward the loading dock, using the shadows to mask his presence, Tolstoy close behind him. He stopped and listened. There was no sound from inside the warehouse on the other side of the high wall. Only the whistling of the wind in the trees disturbed the silence outside.

Still, the soldier wondered how many hardmen were hiding on the other side of the wall. This time they weren't expecting him. He hadn't told anyone that he was coming here, not even Brognola.

There was a leak in the support system the Russians had provided. He wasn't sure who was passing on information about his movements to Donielev, but somebody had to have told the hit men where he was.

Irina Tolstoy? He looked at the woman. No, she was exposing herself to as much danger as him.

How did Donielev know about his movements so quickly? There was only one possibility. Lena Kurilov.

Tolstoy and he had argued about it on their way to the warehouse.

"I can't imagine her spying for Donielev," Tolstoy had asserted. "But I will confront her." Concerned, she added, "Lena is no traitor."

"What about Donielev? Would you say the same for him?"

She shook her head. "That's a good point. Even if the bomb may someday be aimed at Russia, someone like Yuri Donielev doesn't care what happens to anyone else but himself."

She brought up another issue. "Have you decided who the buyer is?"

Bolan told her that he was putting his money on Tehran. The Iranians had the funds and the desire to control the Middle East with the threat of a nuclear device. The madman of Baghdad had chemical warheads at his disposal. Even though the Iraqi dictator knew that if he unleashed even one of the warheads, the Americans would immediately retaliate with a so-called clean nuclear device that could obliterate a small area, Hussein had refused to dispose of the horror weapons.

The soldier suspected that as much as Hussein wanted nuclear weaponry, he didn't have the money to compete with the Iranians for the plutonium or the scientists capable of putting together a nuclear weapon.

As far as the North Koreans were concerned, he suspected that they already had such a weapon. Or if they didn't, they were close to manufacturing one.

No, the Iranians were busy buying all kinds of military hardware from the partially disbanded Russian forces. They'd already acquired submarines, fighter jets, as well as rifles and pistols. The Russians had said no when the Iranian negotiators inquired about purchasing surplus nuclear devices, even when the representatives of their fundamentalist neighbors offered the equivalent of a hundred million American dollars in hard currency.

From what Brognola had told him on their flight, the Russians didn't trust the Shiites who controlled Iran. Not with the ingredients for a nuclear bomb. Not when they were their closest non-Muslim neighbors.

There were a lot of unanswered questions floating in his mind. As far as Bolan was concerned, the first was the most important one: how to stop Donielev's gang from delivering the nuclear experts and their material to the Iranians?

First he had to find them.

Perhaps one of Donielev's men would know. All he had to do was to capture one of them and keep him alive until he talked, which was easier said than done. From what he had seen, Donielev's gang, like most Russian mafia groups, had a code of loyalty. They would rather be killed than reveal anything.

His reflections faded quickly as he saw the night shadows on the wall begin to move. He pointed them out to Tolstoy and signaled for her to take a position against the wall.

The shadows turned into four thickset men carrying 5.45 mm AK-74 carbines, and they were heading for a Volvo parked alongside the warehouse loading dock.

The quartet stared at the parked military vehicle and stopped, turning their heads, searching for the driver.

Bolan stepped away from the wall and held his 9 mm Beretta in a two-handed grip.

One of the sentries sensed the soldier's presence and turned, bringing his weapon to bear. Before he could get off a shot, several rounds tore into his mouth and out the back of his neck.

Bolan knew the source of the thug's death—Irina Tolstoy.

But there was no time to offer compliments. The other three mafia fighters required his immediate attention. The Executioner whirled to his left and out of the direct path of the aimed rifles. Muzzle-flashes winked as all three hardmen fired at his last position.

Bolan holstered the Beretta. He had to answer that type of firepower with more heat. Swinging up the Skorpion he returned the fire from his new location, hosing the space in front of him from left to right with a carefully placed burst from the Skorpion.

One of the attackers spasmed in pain as hot metal tore his throat to shreds and shoved him back against the wall. A second gunner dropped his AK-74 and clutched his midsection, trying to close the cavity that had suddenly appeared.

The third sentry rushed at the Executioner, crazed by the burning lead that had shattered his neck and right shoulder.

Bolan sensed Tolstoy next to him. He could hear the steady pull of her Tokarev's trigger as she unleashed a pair of shots at the charging thug.

Turning his Kalashnikov submachine gun on her, the sentry started to unleash the carbine's awesome firepower. She stopped his movement with two lead blasters that chewed into his chest, shoving him backward. Tripping, the gunner fell to the ground, writhing with pain.

The woman ended his agony with a well-placed single bullet that drilled into his temple and lodged in his brain.

Leaving Tolstoy to check that the four hardmen were really dead, Bolan quickly scanned the area for additional sentries. Either there were no others on the perimeter of the compound or they were waiting in ambush inside.

Moving among the shadows, the soldier worked his way around to the solid wooden gates that barricaded the compound.

Pushing a hand against one of the heavy doors, Bolan saw it move. He pushed a little harder. The well-oiled hinges prevented the gate from squealing as it opened. He moved inside the walled area, then waited and listened carefully. The silence was almost overwhelming.

The Executioner decided to move to the rear of the building and try to enter through a back door.

Using the darkness for cover, Bolan worked his way cautiously against the stone wall of the building. At the corner he exposed his head briefly to check for waiting assassins.

No one.

He wandered into the large open storage area on the ground floor, which was empty.

Streaks of oil were evidence that vehicles had once been parked in here. Only shuffled dust remained where once stacks of boxes had to have stood. A piece of baling wire and slivers of wood from crates were all that remained. It was as if the entire gang had suddenly decided to remove what they had stored here and abandon the warehouse.

Something was wrong. Nobody in Russia, no matter how rich, just abandoned a building. It was contrary to their culture. Families lived in the same apartments, companies occupied the same factory buildings, for as long as they could. Even the wealthy had difficulty finding decent housing in the overpopulated capital. But Donielev and his men had just walked away and left the warehouse open to plunderers who would steal anything that was removable.

As he continued his careful journey to the rear door, Bolan tried to make sense out of the situation.

He substituted the Beretta for the Skorpion submachine gun. Slinging the strap of the Czech weapon over his left shoulder, he wrapped his large hand around the autoloader and tried the door handle. It turned easily and the door swung open.

Holding his Beretta in front of him, the soldier opened a small door and found the answer to the riddle.

The door led to a small office. Inside, four bodies lay in a neat row on the floor.

Bolan moved from the office through a rear door into a hallway. Five more bodies, their faces and chests shredded by slugs fired at close range, were sprawled in the corridor. The walls and ceilings were stained with their blood.

Moving cautiously down an adjacent hallway, he found himself in front of a freight elevator. Moving up the stairs that paralleled the lift, Bolan knew he would find additional corpses.

He wasn't disappointed.

One thick-necked hardman, his eyes staring permanently at the ceiling, was sprawled at the top of the first landing.

Searching the immediate area, the Executioner found two more bodies. He was puzzled. These people weren't amateurs. It would have taken a troop of trained gunmen to kill them all.

Bolan checked the next landing for additional bodies, and found a dozen more.

The warehouse was a cemetery. A force large enough to slaughter more than twenty trained mafia gunners had invaded the building.

Returning to the main floor, he searched carefully for clues. A possible answer to the riddle was printed in Russian on a sheet of paper he found next to one of the bodies.

Bolan couldn't read Russian as well as he could speak it. He shoved the paper into a pocket to have Tolstoy translate it later. Then he searched the rest of the room.

Several small plastic bags of illegal drugs had fallen behind a stack of crates. He slit one open with his combat knife and tasted a few specks: heroin, probably grown in Russia or one of the former Soviet republics.

Drugs were a five-billion-dollar industry. Thousands of soldiers had become addicted to heroin during the course of the Afghanistan war. The poppy derivative had been easily available on every corner of Kabul, the Afghan capital.

Although most of the heroin stayed in the various former Soviet republics, enough was exported to Eastern and

Western Europe, as well as to the United States and Canada, to make Russia a major player in the international drug business.

According to Hal Brognola, the Azeris who had moved to Moscow from their native Azerbaijan claimed the narcotics business as theirs exclusively.

He heard a noise from the other room and whirled. Through the open doorway, he could see Tolstoy talking into a wall telephone. After she hung up, the woman walked into the open area and stared at the bodies.

Bolan handed her the paper he had found. "What does this say?"

"It's a warning from the Azeri mafia about trying to take over their drug business." She looked grim as she studied the paper. "There are also comments about staying out of businesses that belong to others."

"A gang hit?"

"I think so," she replied. "One of the men outside wasn't dead. I convinced him to talk."

"Did he say anything useful?"

"He wasn't fully coherent. But from what I could make out, he and the others outside got a call to rush here."

"He explain why?"

"Not completely. Something to do with Donielev deciding to shut down operations in Moscow for a while."

"Did Donielev order the killings?"

"The man died before I could ask."

It was an old game among mafia gangs in the United States, leaving nobody behind who could be dangerous.

"What about the ransom?"

"I just called the president's aide. He was getting ready to pick up the money at the American Embassy and deliver it himself." She paused. "I told him I would handle it. He was grateful. So now we go to Sokolniki Park."

"This could be a setup," Bolan warned.

"How will we find out if we don't go there?"

"You're right. You drive."

"We have a stop to make," she reminded him.

"Where?"

"To pick up the money."

Then she added, "And ask them to return the car to its owner—with a full tank of gas."

Despite the surroundings, Bolan had to smile. The Russian woman was the most ethical person he had encountered in a long time.

As they pulled away from the warehouse, the Executioner wondered if he had been a witness to the start of mafia gang warfare.

If so, good riddance.

He just hoped he'd be able to lend them a hand.

12

Yuri Donielev stamped his feet impatiently as he peered into the darkness of Sokolniki Park. The six-hundred-acre tract, set in the middle of Moscow, was normally filled with the sounds of thousands of Muscovites, grateful to escape the harsh realities of their daily lives.

But at ten in the evening, it was deserted. No one dared walk through it alone. Muggers and rapists seemed to be waiting behind every tree, every stand of bushes.

An occasional drug addict scurried along one of the pathways, desperately searching the darkness for a dealer who could sell him something to numb his fears and feelings.

Donielev turned to Max Haverford, who sat on a fender of the Mercedes-Benz sports car.

"Where is this messenger with the money?" The former KGB official was furious. "My letter gave explicit instructions."

"Maybe the government changed its mind."

"You don't understand how Russians think," Donielev growled. "It's not even their money. They got it from the Americans."

Besides, he reminded himself, it was time to leave Moscow. At least until he could build a bigger, more powerful organization. The money he got from the Russian government, and from the Iranians, would help him attract the best

talent. A lot better than the weaklings who had let themselves be killed by his rivals.

The command from Khreshchatik still hurt. He had
trusted his former mentor, and the man had turned on him.
Someday soon he would get his revenge.

On Khreshchatik and the others at the luncheon.

"I shouldn't even be here," Haverford commented, in-
terrupting Donielev's thoughts. "It's important nobody
finds out about my involvement in this matter."

"Stop complaining. If you want your share of the money,
you share in the risks, like the rest of us."

Donielev kept looking around, trying to peer into the
darkness.

"You've got enough men posted to spot a squirrel,"
Haverford commented.

Donielev had spread twenty of his best marksmen around
the area. He didn't know who would be delivering the ransom.

Maxim Legulin slipped out of the shadows to stand at the
general's side.

He was dressed in a pair of combat jump boots, military
pants and shirt and a thick field jacket.

"Any sign of the messenger?" Donielev asked.

"Nothing, General. Perhaps he sensed this was a trap and
is not coming."

Donielev considered the comment. "We will wait another half hour, then leave. Meantime make sure the men
are alert."

Legulin saluted, then turned and moved back toward a
stand of trees where he and two of his men had been waiting.

The former general turned back to the open car door.

Haverford smiled at him from inside the vehicle. "Pa-
tience. If not tonight, the money will be ours in a few days.
I'll stop by my apartment and pack a bag. Then I'll drive to
your house and leave my car there."

Donielev nodded. The business would soon be completed. There was a slight change of plans, which he hadn't bothered sharing with Haverford. As they had planned, he would fly to meet Haverford, then return with the Iranian's money—alone.

The stately-looking American got out of the rear of the sports car and walked to where he'd parked a Jaguar. The foreign car had cost Haverford more than a hundred thousand in American currency.

"Nice car," Donielev commented, studying the low profile of the British-made vehicle.

"You can have it as a gift after we finish our business."

The former KGB general nodded. The American wouldn't be needing his fancy car. Not unless it was possible to drive around in Hell.

Even as a child, Donielev remembered how much he hated sharing with other children. He hadn't changed. He wanted all of the money for himself.

THE MAFIA SUBCHIEF paused to sneak a cigarette. As he lit the strong-tasting Turkish tobacco, Legulin felt something brush against his neck. A mosquito? No, this was something hard.

Suddenly he knew what it was. The muzzle of a gun.

"How many men are there?"

The whispered question seemed to come out of the night itself.

The hardman tried to turn his head to look at the man holding the weapon.

"Move an inch and you're dead," the whisperer promised. "Where are the others?"

"I have two men behind the trees to my right."

"How many others are there?"

Controlling his fear, the man replied, "Just the three of us."

"Wrong. There were at least three others. They're all dead."

Bolan stepped out of the shadows and faced the hardman. Dressed in his blacksuit, his face covered with camouflage makeup, he knew he looked like a creature from Hell.

Tolstoy and he had confronted a trio of armed men when he drove the GMC panel truck with the cases of money through the wooded area. As the two of them got out of the van, one of the hardmen had raised the Tokarev he gripped in his fist. Before the gunner could get off a shot, Bolan had taken him out of the play with a burst from the silenced Beretta 93-R.

The other two hardmen began to bring their Uzi machine pistols into target acquisition. A pair of 3-round bursts from the Beretta tore holes in their chests before either man could unleash a single shot.

Bolan instructed Tolstoy to recon the area. Before she moved into the brush, he noticed that she knelt and plucked a long-bladed combat knife from one of the bodies.

"AGAIN," BOLAN ASKED the mafia subcommander, "how many others are there?"

"About twenty," the man replied.

"Where?"

"All around us." He regained his bravado for a moment. "You can't escape. The ambush was too well planned."

As he spoke, the former KGB officer worked a long, thin blade from the sheath attached to his right forearm. Crafted from a quarter-inch-thick slab of high-carbon stainless steel, the knife had eleven inches of shaving-sharp cutting edge.

Grasping the steel hasp, the Russian saw his opportunity to strike when Bolan turned his head briefly to study the area around him.

Thrusting the point of the blade at his adversary's throat, Legulin tried to sever the main neck artery.

Bolan saw the blade coming at him and instinctively pulled the trigger of the Beretta, drilling two slugs into his attacker's face.

In a fit of fury and frustration, the hit man tried to shout a warning, but Bolan clamped a hand over his mouth and wrestled the dying man to the ground.

TOLSTOY MOVED SLOWLY through the brush, being careful not to make unnecessary noises. In her right hand she gripped the Tokarev pistol. In her left was the confiscated combat blade.

The American had wanted her to do recon. She planned to do much more.

Two shadows detached themselves from the wide tree in front of her. Pausing, she watched the two hardmen start to move in the opposite direction, Skorpion submachine guns held ready in their hands.

She moved swiftly toward the nearer of the pair, then thrust the point of the combat knife into his back, carefully twisting her hand as she pushed the steel blade in to sever vital internal organs.

Gulping for air his slit lungs couldn't contain, the gunner fell against the tree trunk. His partner turned his head and stared at him.

He sounded concerned as he whispered, "Valery, is something wrong?"

The red-haired colonel pushed her autoloader into the second man's neck and fired a round, stepping sideways to avoid the sudden spring of blood that jumped from the gaping hole.

The echo of the shot reverberated through the trees. She knew men would rush to her position, ready to kill the intruder. It was time to move to a different location.

BOLAN HEADED for the shadows. As his eyes became accustomed to the dark, he could see the shapes of men and the weapons they were holding.

He checked the extra clips in the pocket of his zipper jacket. Two full magazines. Not enough for a full-scale battle.

He leaned down and scooped up the Uzi pistols the dead men had been carrying, as well as the pair of 30-round clips taped together on a canvas belt around one man's waist. Where they were going, they had no need of weapons or ammunition.

Bolan checked the clips in the Israeli-made 9 mm auto-pistols. They were full. Sixty rounds of death, ready to be dispatched. He slung the weapons over a shoulder, and decided to stick with his own Uzi SMG.

Easing the Applegate-Fairbairn combat blade from its sheath, the soldier tucked it inside his canvas belt and moved against the remaining hit men.

DONIELEV DECIDED the American wasn't coming.

"Maxim!" he called out to his lieutenant.

No one answered.

Donielev swore loudly. "Where the hell are you, Maxim?"

The only response he got was a loud "woosh" sound from behind the trees. The ex-KGB general recognized the noise. It was the sound of a suppressor-equipped weapon being fired.

He grabbed the AKSU-74 SMG from the floor of his Mercedes-Benz 500 SL sports car and dived to the safety of the dirt road.

The American had arrived.

Donielev promised himself that the intruder would never leave the park alive. If one of his men didn't get him, he would.

The mafia leader decided to move to a thick stand of trees on his right. From behind them he could see anyone approaching.

Checking the area swiftly, he could see no one. In a sudden burst of energy, he threw himself across the dirt road and into the woods.

13

Bolan didn't believe in needless killing, but he would kill an enemy when it was necessary to the mission or to his own survival. This night he had no choice. To leave live gunners behind him would be akin to courting disaster. When he encountered a mafia gunner, he made sure the man wouldn't get up.

Suppressing the muzzle noise of a high-powered weapon didn't have the same effect as silencing it. There was still a clearly audible sound.

The soldier turned and moved behind a wide tree as the retort of the Uzi round echoed softly.

He could hear the handful of surviving mafia hardmen yelling in Russian.

"He's over there, where Georgi is hidden," one of them called.

"After him. Kill him."

Bolan knelt and braced the Uzi against his hip, then set the extra weapons and clips on the ground next to him. He started to unhook the grenades from the canvas belt around his waist, then decided they were just as accessible there as they would be on the ground.

The first of the mafia horde charged toward him, spraying lead from his Skorpion SMG randomly in front of him.

Bolan waited until the hardman came closer, then shredded his abdomen with a burst of rounds from the Uzi. To his right the soldier could see a pair of men trying to sneak past him. A short burst of explosive fire punched into their chests and put them down.

There were still at least six more gunmen to deal with, Bolan decided, judging from the sounds coming out of the wooded area.

Three of the enemy gunners tried to use the trees as cover. Hoping that Tolstoy wasn't in the vicinity, Bolan grabbed one of the three frag grenades, waited for the hardmen to come closer, then yanked the pin on a bomb. Counting quickly to ten, he lobbed the grenade at the trees ten yards ahead and lay flat on the ground.

The ear-shattering explosion tore branches and leaves from nearby trees and proved to be deadly for the enemy forces. Gathering his equipment, Bolan moved cautiously forward.

Two gunmen were dead. One was headless, and the other was riddled with pieces of shrapnel.

The Executioner heard groans from behind one of the trees. A large, stocky hardman lay in the bushes, trying to hold his ruined midsection together. Bolan knelt beside him.

"Where is Donielev?"

"I don't know," the hardman gasped. "Stop the pain. Please stop the pain."

"Where are the scientists?"

"They left today."

"To go where?"

"Azer...azerbai..."

"Azerbaijan?"

"Yes." The man was on the verge of unconsciousness.

"When is Donielev joining them?"

"I don't know. American...took...them."

Max Haverford?

"What American?"

"Please stop the pain!"

"What American?" Bolan repeated.

But the mafia hardman was past hearing.

In the distance the Executioner could hear the terrified calls of the surviving gunners as they realized many of their comrades were dead or missing. Sounds of their flight through the brush were clearly audible.

"Come back here, you cowards," said a voice that Bolan had heard shouting orders earlier.

In response he heard several car engines starting. Cars burned rubber in their drivers' haste to escape the scene of death.

There was one more response. From Bolan.

"Are you too afraid to stay and fight?" he challenged.

Bolan emerged from the woods and saw the ex-KGB general hiding behind his Mercedes.

"I know you, American. I've read a file on you. You are the one they used to call Mack Bolan, the Executioner, the insane assassin from the United States. You're supposed to be dead."

"Now it's your turn to die," Bolan replied. "Unless you tell me where to find the missing professors."

"You first," Donielev yelled as he stepped from behind his car, firing the Skorpion submachine gun in his hands until it was empty. Donielev dropped behind the small sports car to reload.

But the soldier was no longer in that position. Battle-seasoned, he knew better than to give the enemy a clear target. He had jumped to the right and had focused the Uzi on where the former KGB officer had stood.

"I have a gift for you," Donielev yelled.

The Executioner didn't reply.

"Look at what I found trying to kill me," Donielev shouted, and stood, holding a hostage in front of him.

Irina Tolstoy was struggling to free herself from a neck grip.

Donielev laughed almost hysterically. "She thought she could sneak up on someone with my experience and kill me from behind. Now she dies."

"What kind of deal do you want?"

"I want the money."

The Executioner hoped he'd understood the between-the-lines message from Brognola. "When you release the woman."

Donielev thought, then whistled loudly. A pair of hardmen started to emerge from the wooded area.

"Wait there," the ex-KGB general ordered.

The men stopped.

"Where is the money?"

"Nearby, in a van," Bolan replied.

"Okay. I drive the Mercedes. These two men get the van and drive it. When I get in, I will let the woman go."

Bolan knew the gang leader was lying. He had no intention of letting Tolstoy live. But as long as she was still alive, there was always the chance she could get away.

"Deal," he agreed.

Donielev signaled the two hardmen to get the van. The pair disappeared, then emerged in a few minutes, driving the panel truck. They pulled up behind the sports car.

Bolan shouted a question. "What about the scientists?"

"I'll let the government know where to find them." Bolan knew Donielev was lying, but there was nothing he could do about it.

Moving backward, the Russian mafia chief reached back and opened the front door of the Mercedes.

Bolan watched for the first sign of a double-cross, his Uzi gripped tightly in his hands.

Donielev kept an arm around Tolstoy's neck as he slid inside the car. Then, with a sudden burst of energy, tried to pull her into the Mercedes.

Bolan unleashed a pair of shots at Donielev's forearm, winging him. Roaring in pain, the ex-KGB general released his grip. Tolstoy threw herself away from the car and onto the dirt road, then rolled to the grass at the side.

The Executioner fired a burst at the driver's-side window, gouging rivulets in the bulletproof glass.

The sports car raced down the park road, followed by the van, away from the source of death and toward the city streets.

Bolan started to run for the parked mafia vehicles, then realized Donielev had too much of a head start. He turned to go to Tolstoy, but she was already on her feet, brushing the dirt and grass from her face, arms and body.

He looked around the area. The police would have a field day trying to unravel how so many mafia hardmen had gotten killed. If they were like American cops, they'd come up with a pat conclusion: a shoot-out between two rival gangs.

"I thought he hadn't heard me," she said in apology.

"Don't worry about it. Are you all right?"

"The only thing that is hurt is my pride," she admitted.

"A highly overrated commodity," Bolan said as he led her toward the parked cars.

14

Bolan had dropped Tolstoy at her apartment building and driven the beige Volvo he had found in the park to his hotel to pick up his belongings.

A large car—a Russian-manufactured Chaika—filled with four hard-looking men was waiting across the street from the entrance to the building.

Too many innocent bystanders were on the street for Bolan to make stand there. Instead he drove the borrowed vehicle around the corner and down an alley. Two roughly dressed men were sitting on the ground, their backs against the side of an old building.

Homeless?

Some instinct warned the Executioner that the two were more than men without homes. He drove past them and parked the car at the far end of the alley, then got out and walked into the street. The Uzi hung from a leather sling under his jacket, reloaded and ready.

The Executioner surmised that the men had been there all night. Donielev hadn't had time to contact his men and send them to the hotel. These were the thugs he had suspected would be watching his place after the battle with the BTR-40 APC.

He searched the area for another way to get into the hotel. An adjacent boarded-up office building provided a possible answer.

There was a fire escape above his head, and Bolan jumped and grabbed hold of a folding ladder, pulled it down and scrambled up the steps.

There was a ten-foot gap between the office building's roof and the hotel's. Looking over the edge, he saw the two men, now on their feet and gripping subguns, walking slowly toward the parked vehicle.

Bolan stood at the edge of the roof and jumped, landing on the roof of the hotel without losing balance.

He searched for a door, but the only exit he could find was a heavy metal door that was locked from the inside. His only alternative was the hotel fire escape that faced the alley.

Wondering if he could get inside the hotel without attracting the ambushers below, he moved cautiously down the metal steps. His room was on the sixth floor, five levels below the roof.

As he headed down, Bolan decided he could force open the window on the sixth floor, apologize if there was anyone in the room and make his way to the room where his clothes and extra gear were stored.

The soldier stopped at the seventh floor, looking down into the alley. The two men had searched the car, walked into the street and looked in both directions, and were now returning.

One of them looked up at the hotel building. Spotting Bolan's semihidden form, he tapped his partner's arm.

Both men turned their weapons toward him.

Resigned to the battle, Bolan pulled the Uzi from under his jacket and dropped to the open-metal frame of the fire-escape landing.

The two hunters on the ground below unleashed waves of lead in his direction. The metal framing acted as a shield for the warrior, deflecting heated metal and sending the rounds ricocheting in every direction.

Poking his weapon through the metal frame, the Executioner traced the movements of the two gunners, then gently squeezed the Uzi's trigger as he moved the subgun slowly from left to right.

It was too dark to ascertain how much damage he had done. Both shooters fell to the ground, dropping their Skorpions as their bodies shivered.

Bolan waited. The shivering stopped, and both men became still. If they weren't dead, they were good actors, the soldier decided. It didn't matter. For the moment they weren't going to interfere with his plans.

He turned and forced open the large window. Clothing was draped over an easy chair and on the bed.

Bolan listened for sounds of life. There were none. Whoever occupied the room was out for the moment. Closing the window, he moved to the door, opened it and checked the hallway.

Empty.

Moving slowly, he stopped at the door to his room and listened. No sounds came from inside.

He started to insert the room key in the lock, then spotted the puttylike substance pressed into the doorjamb, all the way down to the carpet. A thin, almost invisible wire ran under the door.

Bolan recognized the setup—plastic explosive, with a trip trigger, set to detonate when the door was opened.

The soldier was glad he had found the device before an innocent maid, coming to make the beds, tried to open the door.

The only way to deactivate the device was from inside the room.

Bolan went to the door next to his and knocked on it.

"Yes?" somebody inside called out in English.

"American Embassy," Bolan replied.

He could hear movement, then the door opened. A short, fat man in his early fifties stared at him.

"Something wrong?"

Bolan didn't have time for explanations. He pointed the Uzi at the now-terrified American.

"Not if you cooperate."

The Executioner stepped into the room and closed the door behind him.

"What do you want?" the man blurted.

Bolan glanced at the man's companion, naked under the bed covers, then moved to the window.

The dark-haired woman looked terrified. "Did Sergei send you?" she asked in Russian.

"No. Sorry for the interruption."

The woman was already out of the bed, pulling on her scanty attire. The man reached for his pants. Digging into his wallet, he grabbed a number of American bills and handed them to her.

She smiled as she quickly counted the money.

"Thank you," she said as she ran from the room.

Before the American could ask questions, Bolan opened the window and climbed out onto a wide ledge.

"Close the window and don't open your door for at least an hour," he warned.

Carefully stepping along the ledge, Bolan worked his way to the window of his room. Behind him he could hear a window shut and blinds being lowered.

He searched the window frame but he didn't find any plastique.

Trying to open the window, he remembered he had locked it before he had left. He slipped off his jacket and held it against the glass, then used the butt of his Uzi as a hammer.

The glass tinkled and fell onto the carpet inside. Bolan wrapped his hand in his jacket and reached in to unlatch the window frame. Sliding it open, he stepped inside and moved to the door.

The explosive trigger was a simple device. Opening the door to the room set off a small electrical charge that triggered a detonator, which in turn set off the plastique.

Dismantling the device was easy. Bolan carefully freed the wire from the electrical connection, then removed the detonator. Opening the door, he pulled the claylike explosive from the door frame and dropped the components into a wastebasket.

It was time to change locations. But where?

He lifted the phone and called Brognola at his hotel. Briefing the Stony Man Farm head on the events, he asked if there was a safehouse in Moscow he could use.

"You've been busy tonight. My contacts at the embassy say you've got a lot of people mad at you. Especially the mafia types. Did Donielev get the money?"

"Yes. I hope I understood the message on the plane."

"I had the boys at the Stony Man Farm labs coat the bills with a new phosphorus-based compound we developed. Extended exposure to the air will make them start to burn."

"Any word on the missing scientists? I don't think Donielev intended to return them."

"Nothing. How about you?"

"Just that they've left Moscow, or are about to leave."

"I could ask the Moscow police to send extra guards to watch all the airports," Brognola suggested.

"No. That might scare off Donielev and force him to kill them." He was silent for a moment, then added, "I'll think of something."

"Meantime I'll check on a safehouse. Try to hang around for fifteen minutes. I'll call you back."

TEN MINUTES LATER the phone rang. It was Brognola.

"Got you a safe place to stay tonight. I should have something more permanent set up by tomorrow. Pack your stuff and wait at the employees' entrance. A car will pick you up."

"How will I know it's the right car?"

"You'll know."

After packing his bag with clothing, Bolan grabbed it and the canvas battle bag he had hidden behind a loose panel in the closet, and headed for the stairs. Working his way down to the ground level, he saw a sign in Russian indicating the way to the employees' door.

Bolan peered through a small glass pane set in the door and could make out the front end of a Russian jeep, of Korean War vintage, with its engine running.

Despite their bulk, the soldier grabbed both bags in his left hand and used his right hand to grip his Uzi. He shoved the door open with his left elbow against the release bar.

Irina Tolstoy sat behind the wheel of the GAZ-69. She was wearing jeans, a sweater and a leather jacket, looking more like one of the women who patronized one of the fashionable Moscow nightclubs than a former officer of the KGB.

Checking in both directions for ambushers, he swiftly moved to the car. The woman reached across and opened the passenger door. Bolan threw his bags in the back and climbed into the front seat.

"Any trace of the panel truck?" he asked.

"It vanished. So did Donielev. The authorities are searching the city for him."

"Thanks for providing me with a safehouse tonight," he said.

She faced him squarely. "You can use the couch after we talk."

As they pulled out of the alley, Bolan pointed out the large car to her. Tolstoy reached down to the floor, picked up a Skorpion subgun and placed it on her lap.

As they drove past the mafia vehicle, the hardman in the front passenger seat saw Bolan and jerked at the arm of the driver. In a sudden burst of energy the Chaika's engine fired into life, and the vehicle raced after the GAZ.

Tolstoy led them in and out of the small streets that bordered the hotel, then sped toward the wide boulevard ahead. The driver of the Chaika tried to move closer. The colonel weaved expertly in and out of traffic, forcing the enemy driver to use his brakes or risk losing sight of the military vehicle.

Bolan tapped the woman's shoulder and pointed to a small park bordering on the boulevard. "Run up on the sidewalk and jam on the brakes," he ordered.

"Then what?"

"Follow my lead."

Tolstoy looked uncertain, then made a decision. She spun the wheel in the direction of the sidewalk and jumped the curb. Just before she hit a large tree, she rammed her foot on the brakes and the GAZ skidded to a stop.

The Chaika narrowly missed smashing into a lumbering truck as it sped toward the parked vehicle.

Bolan was ready with an M-67 grenade. Knowing it had a delay factor of four to five seconds, he rolled it along the sidewalk as the Chaika jumped the curb.

"Duck!" he shouted, forcing the woman to the floor.

The blast lifted the car into the air. It hung still for a brief moment, then twisted and landed upside down. The two occupants in the front were motionless, their necks twisted and snapped. The two survivors smashed the car windows and crawled out, 9 mm Cobray M-11 subguns gripped in their hands.

Getting to his feet, Bolan balanced the Uzi and waited for his adversaries to see him.

Hate flooding his face, one of the hardmen brought his weapon into target acquisition. Before he could get off a round, Bolan punched him to the ground with a sustained burst.

The second gunner started to crawl away, then suddenly stopped and turned back, his automatic pointed directly at Bolan.

A blistering volley spit from Tolstoy's weapon, shattering the face and neck of the would-be assassin.

Bolan checked the bodies, making sure the hardmen were dead. "You're good with a gun," he said to Tolstoy. "Where'd you learn to shoot like that? Cal Tech?"

She shook her head. "KGB."

"I'll have to remember that."

As she turned and walked back to the GAZ, the colonel replied, "Please do. We are equals on this mission."

Bolan looked at the faceless remains of the mafia gunner she had killed.

She was right.

15

Tolstoy parked the car at the curb, then led Bolan to the front door of her apartment building.

It was an old building, built in the late thirties, the soldier thought. There were none of the cracks of post–World War II, Soviet workmanship showing on the exterior of the structure.

Brestskaya Street was one of the few remaining quiet neighborhoods in Moscow. Located a few miles from the center of the city, there were no all-night bars or gaming casinos that had sprouted in many of the other neighborhoods.

"Before they died, my parents and I lived here. Now I live here alone," Tolstoy said. "I've known our neighbors for most of my life. Even those who were KGB informers."

Slinging the Uzi, Bolan grabbed his bags and followed her to the front door of the building. She reached for the doorknob, then stopped.

"I left the Skorpion in the car. Not a wise thing to do," she said. "My apartment is on the second floor. I'll meet you upstairs."

The soldier set down the bags and started to open the front door, then stopped, his combat sense flaring. Moving to one side of the entrance, he pushed the door open with the muzzle of the Uzi.

A withering spray of 9 mm parabellum rounds shredded the wooden entrance. Another wave of lead ripped out more chunks of wood.

Bolan moved the Uzi to his left shoulder, unholstered the Beretta, set the fire selector to automatic and held the weapon in a two-handed grip.

He didn't know how many men were hiding behind the front door, and there was only one way to find out. Kicking the door open with a foot, he surveyed the area in the blink of an eye, taking in two street types, both armed with automatics.

A quick burst took out both men.

Hugging a wall, Bolan caught sight of movement from behind the stair banister. Shouting a curse in Russian, the huge, bald gunman stood and started to squeeze the trigger of the Makarov automatic he gripped in his large hand.

Before Bolan could nullify the threat, two rounds from Tolstoy's Skorpion churned through the gunner's chest, blowing a huge hole in his back. The dead mafia fighter fell backward against the steps.

Bolan aimed his Beretta at the top of the staircase, trigger finger ready to pull back and empty the clip. Irina Tolstoy appeared at his side, her Skorpion in her hand.

She glanced at the three bodies, then looked at Bolan. "I guess I'll have to have a couple of policemen watch my place until this is all over."

"That could be a good idea," Bolan agreed.

"Come upstairs. We should talk."

Bolan looked at the bodies. "Are you going to call somebody about them?"

"I suppose I'll call the police. I'd prefer to call the trash collectors," she answered, and turned to lead the way upstairs.

MAX HAVERFORD LIT a Cuban cigar with a wooden match. He watched the smoke curling to the ceiling as Yuri Donielev paced the living-room floor of the secluded dacha.

"Relax," Haverford suggested. "It's almost over."

"More than thirty men are dead," Donielev muttered, staring at the bandage that covered his battle wound.

"You were going to get rid of them anyway," the ex-CIA agent reminded the angry man. "Somebody did the dirty work for you."

"I was not getting rid of Federov or Legulin," the Russian growled. "What kind of person is this Belasko?"

Haverford shrugged. "A very dangerous one, based on what's he's already done." He shook his head. "Does it matter?

"I'm flying the two scientists out in the morning to turn them over to the Iranians. And you're getting rid of your holdings. We'll meet in Baku."

"You have the easier job. Delivering the two scientists to the Iranians and collecting the money," the former KGB general commented.

Haverford stared at the Russian, his face covered with disbelief. "Have you ever dealt with the Iranians?"

Donielev hadn't, which was why Haverford was involved. Most of the ex-KGB general's operations had been confined to the Soviet Union and maintaining control of its citizens. Haverford had done business with many of the foreign governments, both while he was with the CIA and afterward.

Without Haverford and his Iranian contacts, the pot would have been fifteen million dollars.

Not a bad sum.

But nothing compared to what Haverford was getting from the Shiites in Tehran. Thirty million dollars, in gold.

Like the men in his gang, the American was expendable. But only after Donielev took possession of the gold. Then Haverford, like the slow-witted street thugs Donielev had recruited, would no longer be useful.

The mafia leader had already planned his temporary exit from Russia. Perhaps a villa in Libya. It would give him the time he needed to rebuild his organization and plan his return to Moscow.

Haverford interrupted his thoughts. "One of my staff has arranged a house in the foothills of the city." Haverford didn't add that Gilal Kurbanov had also arranged to hire a dozen mercenaries to guard the hillside building.

"Leave the address so I know where to meet you," Donielev reminded him.

"I'll also leave the phone number of a place in the Talysh Mountains. If we have any trouble with the Iranians, we'll move to a safehouse in Palikesh, a small village at the bottom of one of the mountains."

"I will be there when the Iranians arrive and we exchange the researchers for the money."

"Sounds cut-and-dried," Haverford agreed. "Afterward we split the money. I take off for my home, and you head for wherever you've decided to go." He smiled at the Russian. "See? There's nothing to worry about."

"There's this Michael Belasko. He's still alive."

"So are we. You worry too much, Yuri. Relax. Enjoy your success."

The former KGB general stopped his pacing and stared at his guest. Smiling, he said, "You're right. This is your last night in Moscow for a while. We should go out and have fun."

Haverford looked suspicious. He knew about Donielev's reputation with women. "What did you have in mind?"

"We'll dress up and go gambling."

He walked to the door and shouted for the guards.

"And just to make sure we are not bothered, we'll take three men with us."

THE APARTMENT WAS pitch-black. Bolan had settled down on the couch, when the bedroom door opened.

"Are you awake?"

"Yes," he said, sitting up. "Something wrong?"

"I was just thinking. We keep waiting for tips on where to find Donielev, instead of hunting for him."

"Got any ideas?"

"Donielev is supposed to be a compulsive gambler. When he isn't womanizing, he spends his spare time at one of the new casinos that have opened in Moscow."

Bolan was beginning to get the idea. "You think we ought to go and search for him there?"

"He prefers the Casino Royale, the most expensive of all the gambling rooms in the city." She became quiet, then said, "It will give you a chance to see him in person. What do you think?"

"I think we should give it a try."

"Good," she said, and turned on the overhead light in the living room.

Bolan stared at the vision in the doorway. For a moment he didn't recognize the attractive woman in the deep red velvet evening gown. He had never really looked at her. She was an exceedingly handsome woman.

She might be an ace security official, Bolan told himself silently, but she was a beautiful woman.

"How long will it take you to get ready?"

"Give me ten minutes," he said, grabbing his suitcase and slipping into the bathroom.

A few minutes later, dressed and feeling secure with the Beretta hanging from its shoulder holster, Bolan let the security colonel put a gloved hand through the crook of his arm as they left the apartment.

This could be a night of fun, he reminded himself, if it wasn't business.

And the business at hand was death.

THE CASINO REMINDED Bolan of Las Vegas. Crap tables were lined up next to tables of roulette. Blackjack games were everywhere, and for the more affluent there were four baccarat tables.

The sumptuous palace built for Czar Nicholas I in the mid-1800s had been converted into a giant moneymaking machine for the casino's owners. Hundreds of players, eager to lose their money at one of the tables or in the numerous slot machines, crowded into the giant room.

The dealers, both men and women, were wearing formal attire. With stolid expressions, they called for bets and announced when bets were no longer acceptable.

Behind each of the biggest spenders stood several cold-faced, streetwise types, their eyes checking every movement in the huge room. Bolan would bet that under their oversize dinner jackets, the hard-faced toughs carried one or more automatic weapons, cocked and ready to thunder at the release of a safety.

Seated at the farthest baccarat table was a stocky bald man who kept glaring at the cards as the dealer tossed them at him. Donielev.

He looked older than in the photograph Brognola had shown him, but it was the same man. The expensive suit the man wore didn't mask his cold viciousness.

"He doesn't look happy," the warrior whispered back.

"Donielev hates losing."

The ex-KGB general turned to a stately tall man standing behind him. He signaled him to move closer, then whispered something. The other man shook his head, then changed his mind and reached into an inner pocket of his suit jacket. Withdrawing a thick wad of American hundred-dollar bills, he handed them to the seated man.

The tall man looked familiar, then Bolan remembered the photograph Brognola had shown him.

Maxwell Haverford.

Tolstoy saw Bolan staring at Donielev's companion. "I don't know him," she commented in a low voice.

The Executioner told her. He could almost smell the corruption from across the room.

Haverford raised his head, as if some silent whistle had warned him to look around the room, and saw Bolan staring at him. The soldier could sense the former CIA man was trying to find his face in his memory bank. Then he gave up and tapped the seated ex-KGB general on the shoulder. When Donielev turned his head, the American gestured for them to leave. The Russian was about to argue, then saw the determined expression on the other's man face and gathered up the small stack of chips in front him.

As the two walked toward the doors, a well-dressed young man stopped them. Bolan didn't recognize him, but Irina Tolstoy did.

"Viktor Lasky, one of the president's aides. He presided over the meeting with your Hal Brognola yesterday."

As they watched, the government official chatted with the two men. Finally Haverford reached into an inner pocket and took out a thick envelope. He smiled as he handed it to Lasky, then led Donielev out of the gaming room. Three bodyguards followed the pair out.

"If information about the law enforcement conference is leaked to these criminals, we will know the source," Tolstoy commented.

She looked around the room. "The subways are filled with homeless people who do not have enough money to buy food, and these idiots keep throwing money away in rooms like this all over Russia." She sighed. "Democracy is a wonderful thing. But in these early stages, it is still unfair."

"I could take out Donielev right now, but killing him wouldn't rescue the missing scientists and the plutonium.

"Can I buy you a drink, Colonel?" Bolan added.

"I'll let you. Perhaps a glass of wine. Then back to my apartment. We have a busy day tomorrow."

16

Bolan and Tolstoy left the casino and got into the GAZ, which was parked around the corner.

As they drove away, Yuri Donielev turned to his companion.

"The woman in that transport. I know her. Irina Tolstoy. But are you sure that man is Mack Bolan?"

"I'd bet money on it. The Company has had run-ins with him before," Haverford commented. "Getting rid of him would solve some of your problems."

The former KGB general leaned over and whispered something to the driver, who turned to glance at the other three mafia soldiers in the limousine.

"The boss says there's a bonus for each of us if we take care of the couple who just drove off in the GAZ." He looked at Donielev. "How are you going to get home?"

The ex-KGB director signaled a cab to come closer.

"You just concentrate on catching up with that GAZ," he said coldly.

TOLSTOY CLOSED HER EYES and leaned her head back on the passenger seat.

Bolan's voice made her sit up straight.

"Not to alarm you, but I think that black limo is trying to catch up with us."

She turned her head. The American was right. She glanced at him. He had moved the snub-nosed 9 mm Uzi from under his jacket to his lap. A pair of spare clips for the Israeli-made weapon was on the car floor.

She reached into her purse for her Tokarev pistol.

The long, flashy black limo kept coming closer to the GAZ, its engine straining to catch up with the vehicle.

Bolan turned his head quickly. He could see the face of the driver behind him. The man sitting next to him was making wild hand gestures urging him to get closer.

Tolstoy looked at Bolan. "What should we do?"

"Can you squeeze in front of me and take the wheel?"

"I can try," she replied.

Forcing herself on his lap, the woman wriggled her way toward the driver's door. Bolan shifted slightly and let her take possession of the steering wheel.

"Put your feet on mine," he said.

She followed his instructions. As he felt her feet above his, he pulled away and let her control the gas and brakes. Then he slid over to the passenger side of the car and opened the window. In his hand he held the suppressed 9 mm Uzi he had concealed beneath his dinner jacket.

Leaning out of the window, he started to shoot at the front tires of the limousine.

"Get your speed up," he shouted to Tolstoy.

She followed his orders, and as he expected, the limo increased its speed to try to overtake them.

The Executioner wrapped his hands around two of the grenades on his belt.

"Let them catch up with us," he ordered.

A look of surprise crossed Tolstoy's face, but she did as she was told and eased up on the gas pedal.

"Pull all the way to the left," Bolan snapped. "I want them to come up on my side."

She glanced at the grenades in his hands and began to understand the plan.

"When I yell 'step on it,' I mean right away and move like a bat out of hell," he added.

Spinning the steering wheel, she pulled into the far left lane.

As Bolan had expected, the limo driver moved up on the right side of the GAZ, and guns were pushed out of opened windows.

Bolan didn't wait. He jerked the M-67 grenades free, pulled the pins, counted to five and tossed the bombs into the limousine.

Tolstoy and he could hear yelling from the vehicle as the hardmen fumbled for the grenades.

"Step on it!"

The colonel floored the gas pedal, and the GAZ raced ahead.

Bolan saw a side street on the left.

"Pull into the street and stop the car," he ordered.

As they got out of the vehicle, they saw the fierce burst of flame lighting the area behind them. The shock waves from the explosion shattered nearby windows, and a shower of metal and glass fragments rained down on them.

"Time to get out of here," he said, as he got back in the GAZ.

He hoped the message to Donielev would be clear: time was running out for him and his kind.

THE PHONE in the hotel suite rang. Brognola grabbed the receiver and raised it to his ear.

"Yes?" he said.

"Is it safe to talk?" Bolan asked.

"I doubt it. This is Russia," Brognola growled.

"I'll be brief. If you don't hear from us for a few days, don't worry. The money's in their hands now. But no researchers yet. The big man hasn't left town yet. We ran into him at a local casino. He sent his boys after us. but the gag exploded in their faces."

The head Fed understood. "Sounds like you had a busy night. Need anything from this end?"

"Two things. See if you can find out anything about my tour guide's assistant. She may be the problem."

"What's the second item?"

"Donielev. Can you find out where he lives?"

"Shouldn't be too hard. Yuri doesn't have a lot of friends in Moscow. He's forced his way into businesses other mafia groups have run for years. I'll ask our locals to worm his home address from one of them."

Brognola scribbled a note to himself. Lena Kurilov, the young lieutenant who worked for Colonel Tolstoy. He'd ask the intelligence people at the embassy to check into it. And find out what rat hole Yuri Donielev used as a home.

"If you need anything, call me at the embassy," Brognola said. "I'll leave the information with a man named Jim Hayslip. He's our own local contact."

The soldier understood. Hayslip was part of Brognola's Stony Man Farm team. At least unofficially.

"Got it," Bolan said, and hung up.

Brognola felt relieved. Striker was alive and hot in pursuit of the kidnappers. He opened the door to the corridor.

Two police officers, one in a captain's uniform, were posted outside his door. When he started to exit, the captain stopped him.

"Can I get you something, Mr. Brognola?"

"I'm just going down to the bar for a drink," the big Fed growled.

"I'm afraid we can't permit that," the officer replied with exaggerated politeness.

"Why the hell not?"

"Ever since one of your men was attacked by hoodlums, we have been assigned to protect you."

"The hoodlum was a cop taking on a side job," Brognola reminded the Moscow policeman.

A hint of disgust flashed across the Russian's face. "We know, sir. I'm sure that even in your country there are dishonest policemen."

"What about Belasko?" he said. "Are you guarding him?"

"We would if we could find him. He's not at his hotel."

Brognola knew where Bolan was, but he wasn't about to share that knowledge with anyone who didn't have a need to know.

Like the Russian police captain.

"I still need a drink."

The Russian officer smiled politely. "Tell me what you want, and I will have it brought to you."

The Stony Man Farm chief glared at the uniformed man, then turned and went back into his room, slamming the door behind him. Now he knew what it felt like to be under house arrest. Disgusted, he turned on the small television set in the room and settled down to watching a rerun of an old American soap opera.

LENA KURILOV MADE SURE she wasn't being followed before she entered the boarded-up warehouse. She wore a tight-fitting beaded dress made in Paris, and looked as if she were ready for an evening of fun.

There was a heavy metal door at the bottom of the steps, and she rapped on it as hard as she could.

The bulky man who opened it didn't bother to conceal the Cobray M-11 submachine gun he wore under his loose-fitting dark jacket. For a moment he studied her face in the dim light pouring onto the stairs from behind him. Then he smiled and opened the door wider.

On the other side of the metal barrier was an American-style bar, packed with noisy people. The lighting was dim, the music loud and the cigarette smoke thick.

Young women wore little, desperate to expose as much of their bodies as they thought they could get away with to the expensively clothed men who stared at them through bored eyes.

Only four men looked totally disinterested, three heavy-set toughs who were obviously the bouncers, and the guard at the door. They let the black-haired woman pass.

A well-dressed drunk at the bar tried to grab her around the waist.

"Drink with me," he said, slurring the words.

She tried to pull away but the man held tight.

"I am meeting somebody here," she said coldly, pulling her face away from the man. The odor of whiskey almost overwhelmed her.

"Point him out to me, and I will kill him," the drunk boasted as he started to reach under his jacket.

Two of the three huge bouncers approached the drunk, one of them shoving the muzzle of a submachine gun against the man's right nostril.

"She's with him," the other bouncer said tightly, pointing to a smiling, well-dressed man waiting at a table.

The drunk paled and jumped from his seat at the bar. "I had no way of knowing," he whined to Lena, then repeated the words to the two guards.

Unceremoniously they grabbed the man under the arms and dragged him to the door. Then they opened it and pulled him outside, slamming the door behind them.

The short bald man whose presence had terrified the man at the bar looked pleased to see Kurilov. Yuri Donielev looked up from the glass of French wine he had been sipping and got to his feet.

He waited until she reached the table, then pulled out a chair for her.

"That man at the bar," she said as she sat, "who was he?"

"A dead man, my darling," he replied, leaning across the table and kissing her lightly on her lips.

"You look more beautiful each time I see you," he added, examining the slim body in front of him.

"And you more successful," she replied, squeezing one of his hands affectionately. Then she became serious. "I'm sorry I'm late. Colonel Tolstoy had me on the carpet."

"Anything serious?"

"You."

"Me?" Donielev reacted to her reply with a raising of his thick eyebrows.

"She asked who my rich boyfriend was."

The former KGB official leaned back. "And you said...?"

"He's an older gentleman who makes a fortune bringing hard-to-find goods into Russia and reselling them for a lot of money."

"Older?" Donielev pretended to be hurt by the description. "Perhaps I am too old."

Kurilov squeezed his hand. "Not for me. Anyway the colonel seemed to accept my explanation." She looked into his eyes. "You said it was urgent that we meet in person."

"Again I need your help," he replied, sounding apologetic.

She started to ask a question. "About the two scien—"

Donielev put a finger on her lips to stop her. He looked around to make sure no one had heard her, but there was no one within earshot. The two armed hard-faced men who stood behind him had successfully prevented anyone from approaching his table without his permission.

Haverford had objected when Donielev had told him he had a date with Kurilov, until he explained he was just following up on the American's suggestion.

Mollified, Haverford had agreed to let one of the guards drive him back to the dacha.

"This Belasko who visited your colonel," Donielev said in a low voice. "He could ruin all of our plans."

Kurilov remembered the promises. As soon as the money was in hand, the two of them would leave Russia and move to another country—a more pleasant climate—and enjoy life without any more violence to interrupt them.

Until she had met Donielev, she had struggled to support her fatherless child and herself—a difficult task on the monthly salary of a government employee.

Even with the occasional bribes she received, and the financial gifts from temporary lovers, the young lieutenant had found it almost impossible to survive.

Then Yuri had come into her life. She had known of him before the KGB had been dismantled. He'd been one of the most powerful of the Intelligence department heads.

From what she could learn, Donielev had become a consultant to Russian and American businessmen. His new profession had obviously agreed with him. He always drove the most-expensive imported cars, his clothes were custom-tailored and he had more than a half-dozen buildings and warehouses in Moscow alone.

She remembered how his interest in her—at first a flirtation—had become serious. Lena had been flattered that a former KGB general had fallen in love with her.

The shock of finding out that her new lover was also the head of one of the more notorious mafia gangs in the capital was softened by his explanation that he and she had to do anything to survive the economic chaos of their country.

The gifts he pressed on her—money, a better apartment, money for her grandmother to baby-sit her young child when she was at work or with him, expensive furnishings, imported clothing, an impossibly expensive Swiss wristwatch—made it impossible for her to resist his occasional requests for information about the activities of her ministry.

When the three men from the Obrinsk Research Institute had been brought to her by her superior's nephew to help them find somebody who could set up a fake kidnapping, she immediately thought of Yuri. That one of them, Dr. Polsky, died didn't stop her willingness to help Donielev.

Not when he promised that she would have her own foreign bank account, and that they, and her child, would leave Russia after the remaining scientists and he shared the ransom.

"What can *I* do about this American? He and the colonel are working together," she explained.

"What if they thought they'd found them?"

Kurilov was confused. "What would make them think that?"

Donielev smiled broadly. "You."

The young woman looked surprised. "Me? How?"

"You said Belasko already looks at you with suspicion. Go to him. Tell him you just discovered the man who has been pressing gifts on you is a member of the mafia. Say you are afraid for your life. For the life of your child. That you are positive he plans to kill both of you."

Donielev made it sound as if he had just invented a tale for the black-haired young woman to tell. He didn't add that he had that ending in mind as soon as Belasko and Tolstoy were eliminated.

"You should also say that you know where I was going when I left you tonight."

"Where is that?"

"Remember the small farm in Ramensky, just north of the city, where we spent our first night together?"

"Yes."

She remembered that weekend. They had never left the bedroom.

She looked worried. "I will go to jail."

"Not if your superior thinks you've turned against me. She wants the scientists. And me. Not you."

She looked uncertain. Donielev reached across the table and took her hand again.

"The scientists are being flown out of the country—to Baku—until the ransom money is turned over to us."

He leaned across the table and kissed her lips again.

"Then you and I—and your precious Margaritta—will be on a plane to another place."

He reached into a jacket pocket and took out a small object. Opening her hand, he slipped a ring on her right middle finger.

She stared at the large circlet, which was encrusted with diamonds and rubies. To Lena Kurilov it looked as if it had once belonged to a member of the Russian royal family.

Looking questioningly at the well-dressed man across the table, she started to ask a question.

"It did," he replied as if he had read her mind. "A royal duchess."

The young lieutenant sighed. Even if Yuri was lying to her, she could live for several years on what she would get for selling the ring.

"I think it would be better if I said that to the colonel and let her tell the American."

Donielev thought about her suggestion, then nodded.

Whatever brought Belasko to the farm was the right solution.

As long as it ended in the American's death.

17

The morning sun glared down on the harvested fields as Irina Tolstoy drove the borrowed Volvo close to the large farm in Ramensky and, at Bolan's suggestion, stopped at the side of the pitted asphalt road that ran past the property.

"Let's try to find out how many hunters there are before we walk into the trap," he suggested as he slung the suppressed Uzi over a shoulder.

"Agreed," the woman replied, grabbing the Skorpion subgun. "Do we walk the rest of the way?"

"No. Let's see what we can spot from here before we get any closer."

Tolstoy had shared with him what she knew about the area. The once-thriving agricultural community was still populated by farmers struggling to eke out a living from the abused soil. The days when loyal Soviet photographers and cameramen crowded the government farming commune to record the agricultural successes of the regime had ended with the demise of the empire in late 1991.

Since then, farm families had begun abandoning Ramensky in search of other communities where their survival was more likely. Most of the farms had been taken over by wealthier farmers or companies investing in land.

Like one of the companies Yuri Donielev controlled, according to the colonel's sources.

The Executioner wanted to study the farm from a distance, rather than just rush in with blazing weapons. If the scientists were there, the appearance of the colonel and him could get them killed.

And he was still suspicious that the call Tolstoy had gotten from her aide had been made to sucker them into a trap. It sounded too pat, too simple.

In his experience nothing had ever come so easily.

Except death.

The colonel's aide had called her apartment with a confession. She had discovered the lover she thought was just a successful businessman was really in the mafia, the very mafia gang that had kidnapped the scientists.

Lena Kurilov had said she thought she knew where the two Obrinsk researchers were being held—at a farm her lover owned north of Moscow.

Bolan dug into his canvas bag and retrieved a Leupold 25 power spotting scope, which he rested on the edge of the open window and studied the farm.

The place seemed to be deserted. There was no sign of people or animals around the barn, the bunkhouse or the main building. The only machinery visible was an old military truck that looked as if it had seen more than its share of combat.

The soldier knew better than to rush in without being ready for any surprises. Returning the scope to the bag, he told the colonel to wait until he signaled her.

"We are not even certain the scientists were ever here," she reminded him. "All we know is Yuri Donielev owns this farm and that Kurilov claims he told her last night that he was keeping them here."

"We'll find out when we get inside," he replied.

"So now we go," she said, reaching for the door handle.

Bolan stopped her with a hand on her shoulder. "Something is wrong."

What was wrong became apparent when two bulky men moved out from behind a nearby stand of trees to the right of the farmhouse. Bolan stared at the long tube propped on the right shoulder of one of the pair, then grabbed his Uzi and canvas carryall.

"Get out!" he yelled. "Now!"

Both of the Volvo doors opened, and they dived from the car as the mafia hardman unleashed a PG-7 M HEAT rocket from the RPG-7 launcher.

With a muzzle velocity of 120 meters per second, the 2.25-kilogram missile was capable of penetrating 330 millimeters of armor, which was much thicker than the steel body of the Volvo Bolan had driven.

"Head for the brush," he ordered as he saw the rocket speed at them.

He glanced back and saw the colonel take cover behind a long hedge of bushes. He started to follow her, then hesitated.

Behind him he could hear the rocket tear through the steel skin of the car and destroy the vehicle.

Discarding the empty launcher, the two mafia thugs grabbed for the autoloaders tucked inside their waistbands.

Bolan knew he and Tolstoy were dead if he didn't take the initiative. Dropping the canvas bag, he unslung the Uzi.

Turning to face his adversaries, he stunned the gunners momentarily by racing right at them. Before they could unlimber their weapons, the Executioner washed the area in front of him with a measured burst of 9 mm death.

By the time the Executioner reached the pair, both had fallen to the ground. Cautiously Bolan knelt and checked that they were dead. They were.

He got to his feet and walked back to the bushes where Tolstoy was waiting.

"There may be more," he warned, signaling her to stay put.

He scanned the fields and yard, as he moved slowly around the area. Finally he was satisfied that nobody was hiding—at least outside the farm buildings. He waved for her to join him.

"Stay behind me," he said quietly.

Holding the Uzi in front of him, the soldier eased his way to the small wood-framed building.

"Wait here."

She stopped and let Bolan go ahead. He ducked beneath the nearest window and lifted his head briefly so he could peer inside. The small living room was empty. As he moved from window to window, he risked a peek.

As far as he could determine none of Donielev's men was inside.

He turned and gestured for Tolstoy to join him. She moved to his side, her finger resting against the trigger of her Skorpion subgun.

"Do we go inside now?"

Bolan shook his head. "Not yet."

Something was wrong. He wasn't sure what, but all of his survival instincts warned him to be careful.

They hadn't checked the weather-beaten barn yet, and it was possible that a hardforce lay in wait.

He gestured for the colonel to stand on the other side of the doors. Kicking the nearer one open, he waited for the sound of gunfire.

None came.

The Executioner rushed into the barn and quickly moved to one side. It was safer than being framed by the opened barn door and the bright sun behind him.

Tolstoy followed behind him and, leaning against the wall, she studied the interior. "Nothing in here. No men, no equipment. Not even animals."

"Something is definitely wrong," Bolan agreed. "They must have known we were coming."

Tolstoy nodded in agreement. "Lieutenant Kurilov."

Bolan saw the grim expression on the woman's face. He would hate to be the petite young woman when Tolstoy returned from this mission.

Leading her outside the barn, he reminded her that they were here to find two missing scientists and the plutonium, not to plan her assistant's trial.

Leading the way back to the farmhouse, he paused at the front door. Tolstoy pushed ahead of him and started to grasp the doorknob.

Bolan yanked her hand away. "First we do a check," he ordered.

"Check what? There is no one here. Perhaps they left some clue to their destination inside."

"Perhaps they left something else," he warned.

Bolan moved away from the front door, Tolstoy directly behind him, and stopped when he reached a large tree fifty yards from the house.

"Now we'll find out," he told her.

He jerked one of the M-67 frag grenades from the belt, yanked the pin and spiraled the bomb toward the front door. Then he pulled the woman to the ground as the grenade exploded.

"Plastique, probably," he told Tolstoy as he helped her to her feet. "Not very clever but certainly effective."

"Then they are all gone from here," she replied with frustration.

"Check around the outside. See if you can find fresh tracks of vehicles driving away from here."

Tolstoy was about to protest, but Bolan's stony expression stopped her. She nodded instead and headed toward the fields.

The soldier watched her for a moment, then catfooted to the opening that had been the front door. He listened carefully, then stepped inside and sprayed the room with a sustained burst of 9 mm churners. A huge man wearing a zipper jacket tumbled to the ground, clutching an AKSU-74 submachine gun in his left hand. Blood from his ruptured neck splattered down his shirtfront and drenched his weapon.

Two more hardmen came out of hiding, wildly waving Skorpion machine pistols as they rushed into the room.

There was no time to develop a battle strategy. Bolan spun and washed the pair with the rounds remaining in the Uzi's clip.

A new face appeared at the rear entrance to the front room, a thin man with a scar across his lips that created a permanent smirk.

In his hand was a 9 mm Stechkin automatic.

He spotted the bodies on the floor, looked at the face of the man they'd been sent to kill and brought the Russian pistol into target acquisition.

A pair of searing explosions from behind Bolan tore the thug's chest open. As the mafia gunner fell backward, the Executioner turned and saw Tolstoy, the Skorpion SMG braced against her waist.

"There were car track marks, but they were all coming in, not going out."

As he rammed a fresh clip into the Uzi, Bolan nodded. "I'm not sure we got them all. There's the rest of the house, and the bunkhouse next door."

"I'll check the house," she offered.

Bolan slipped out the back door and moved cautiously toward the smaller building next door. Before he could reach the building, automatic fire began to eat up the ground around him and whined past his ears. The random strays were coming in with sudden accuracy, and he whipped around to find half a dozen mafia hardmen bearing down on him. One bullet tugged at his sleeve, and another traced blood and searing pain across a thigh. The area was alive with angry lead hornets trying to sting him.

He slipped his hand around the Uzi's grip.

It was a solid fighting tool. The Israeli-manufactured SMG weighed less than seven and a half pounds and was only seventeen inches long, from the tip of its short snub barrel to the end of its folded metal stock. Each magazine clipped into its grip held twenty-five rounds of high-velocity ammo. The weapon could be fired one-handed when necessary. Nine-millimeter parabellums hurtled out of the barrel at the rate of six hundred rounds per minute, with a velocity of 1,250 feet per second. Changing magazines took mere seconds.

The attackers rushed from both sides of the bunkhouse, each holding a submachine gun pointed in the Executioner's direction.

Before the gunners could get a bead on him, Bolan plunged into a diving shoulder roll and came up firing, sweeping his Uzi in an arc, left to right and back again. Two of the attackers stumbled as if over invisible wires, sprawling into awkward poses of death. The others scattered, fanning out, falling to the ground. Within a heartbeat they were firing back at him again.

Bolan repeated his evasive maneuver—rolling, rising, firing again and again, matching the hostile fire with calculated bursts. Each time he fired, fewer weapons answered. Finally none of the enemy was alive to reply.

A quick search of the corpses' pockets revealed nothing. Not even a wallet. The Executioner had been hoping that one of the hardmen possessed a clue as to where the scientists had been taken.

He turned away from the bodies when he heard Tolstoy call from inside the house.

"Up here," she called when he'd entered the building.

Bolan checked the clip in his weapon. It was full. He mounted the steps, moving carefully just in case Tolstoy had been taken hostage and was being forced to lure him in.

He found the Russian colonel in one of the rooms, on her knees beside a body. Bolan joined her and looked down. Lena Kurilov's body had been nearly severed in two by bullets.

18

Bolan shook his head. It was hard for him to believe that even someone like Donielev could have ordered this done to another human being.

There was a slight stirring from the body.

"She's still alive," he said.

"Barely," Tolstoy replied, her voice full of anguish.

Bolan knelt beside the dying young woman. "Did Donielev do this?"

"He promised we would go away," she whispered. "He said he loved me."

"He went alone," the Executioner replied. "Where?"

"Not alone. With men," she said, forcing out the words.

He repeated the question. "Where?"

"Baku. A farm," she gasped.

Tolstoy turned to Bolan. "Let her die in peace without making her suffer," she pleaded.

The Executioner ignored her.

"By plane?"

The words came slowly, as if she knew they would be her last.

"Yes, by plane."

Her head fell to one side, and Tolstoy pressed her ear against her aide's chest.

"She's dead."

Helping the colonel to her feet, Bolan led her from the room without saying a word.

Tolstoy stared up at him blankly.

He looked back at her. "What is it?" he asked gently.

"I was thinking about Lena and how all she ever talked about was making a better life for her daughter." She forced back a tear and became all business. "Do you think the two scientists are still alive?"

"Yeah. They're worth more to Donielev alive than dead."

"We must find him and rescue them," she insisted.

"If we can find out where he's gone."

"Let me do some checking," the woman volunteered, and went into the other room to search for a telephone.

She returned moments later, looking grim.

"A group of men left by airplane from Vnukovo Airport. According to the airport director, their destination was Baku."

"That's where Donielev is heading," Bolan said.

"I described him to the director. He was not one of the travelers. There was an American in the group, an older, elegant-looking man."

"Haverford. He must be meeting the Iranians there. We need a plane to get there and stop him."

"Let me make a call."

Tolstoy led him into another room, which was a bedroom. A phone sat on the nightstand. She picked it up and dialed a number.

Ordering someone whose name the soldier couldn't make out to connect her with somebody else, she waited impatiently.

"This is Colonel Irina Tolstoy, of the Ministry of Atomic Energy. You kept me waiting five minutes," she shouted.

Bolan stared at her. This was a side of the woman he had not seen.

"I want a plane fueled and ready to leave for Baku," she ordered.

Apparently the voice on the other end was trying to reason with her.

"Your job is to provide the aircraft, a competent pilot and obtain the proper clearances. Mine is to handle a very delicate mission for the president of the federation."

She checked the antique clock on the wall.

"I am leaving for the airport now. Have the plane ready."

Placing the receiver back on its base, she turned and shook her head.

"No matter how things are changing, this is still Russia, and people still respond to authority. If we are going to get to Baku, we'd better leave for the airport now."

Bolan barely heard her. He was thinking ahead to his confrontation with Donielev.

The Executioner made a decision. "I want you to fly to Baku. Try to find out where Haverford has taken the scientists. Leave a message with the information for Mike Belasko at the American Embassy there. I'll meet you as soon as I can."

The woman looked confused. "Why can't you go with me?"

"There's a rat I need to corner first," he said as he replaced the Uzi's clip.

As they walked out of the farmhouse, Bolan glanced at the twisted metal hulk that had once been a car.

Tolstoy looked at him. "How do we get to the airport?"

The soldier spotted a military truck—a ZIL 157—parked near the barn, stolen by Donielev's men, he assumed, in some raid on a military-equipment depot.

Suddenly he realized they weren't alone. He could almost hear the heightened breathing of hit men hidden inside the cab.

He held up a hand, signaling Tolstoy to stay where she was, then moved slowly toward the truck.

One of the hiding gunners shoved a Skorpion submachine gun out of the passenger window and hosed the area in front of him with a steady stream of scorching lead.

Bolan, anticipating an ambush, dived under the fusillade and rolled toward the truck. His Uzi responded with a carefully placed trio of shots, shattering the face and skull of the gunman.

The driver's door opened, and Bolan could hear the crunching sounds of feet on gravel as a second would-be assassin raced for the rear of the truck. Getting to his feet, the soldier moved in the same direction, crouching to present a smaller target.

A wiry, thin man peered from behind the rear of the vehicle, the assault rifle in his hands spitting flame.

Bolan flattened against the side of the truck. He could feel the edge of a slug streak across his right forearm, leaving a trail of burning pain as it traveled to its destination in the dirt.

Before the soldier could reply, the rifleman rushed past him and jumped inside the truck cab. Bolan, ignoring the pain from the wound, moved cautiously around the vehicle.

Glancing inside the cab, he could see his terrified assailant looking out the opposite window, gripping his carbine tightly in his hands. As if some sixth sense had warned him, the hardman turned his head.

The Executioner drilled three shots into the surprised gunman's chest, killing him instantly. Then he signaled Tolstoy to join him at the truck. The keys were still in the ignition.

Bolan glanced at the roof of the truck cab. A belt-fed 7.62 mm machine gun was mounted on it.

He turned to the colonel. "Can you drive the truck?"

"Of course. I worked two summers as a volunteer truck driver on a farm commune."

She saw the blood on his sleeve. "You're wounded."

"It's only a scratch." He opened the truck door.

Tolstoy reached into her bag and pulled out several adhesive bandages. As she wiped the wound with a clean tissue, she explained, "I always carry several just in case."

She hoisted herself into the cab and caught a quick glimpse of the bloody, twisted corpses of the dead hit men. Leaning out of the opened window, she tried not to vomit.

Bolan saw her expression. He reached inside and tugged the bodies out of the truck, easing them to the ground. Then he slammed the driver's door and pulled himself into the rear of the military vehicle.

"Let's get out of here," he shouted.

Positioning himself behind the mounted submachine gun, he opened a case and found a filled belt of ammo. He fed the webbing into the machine gun and made certain it was ready to fire.

Tolstoy slipped the idling truck into gear, steering the vehicle around in as tight a U-turn as possible.

The Executioner looked back at the house of horrors behind them. In his mind he could still see the broken body of the young woman who had considered the former KGB general her true love. A fatal error, he knew from what he'd read about the degenerate who called himself a man.

As Bolan knew, killing one of his own was nothing new for Donielev. Nothing had changed, except one thing. The Executioner was determined to find him. Alive or dead. And to Bolan it didn't matter which.

THE TRAP HAD BEEN sprung. The American and Irina Tolstoy had taken the bait.

Now he knew where they were.

Sitting in the study of the dacha, Donielev lifted the microphone of the small, powerful transceiver in his home office.

"Mischa," he said to one of his lieutenants, "it's time to get rid of them."

"I'm already in the air. I should be overtaking them in a few minutes," the voice boasted through the shortwave speakers.

A door opened behind the mafia chief, and he turned to look at the bulky young man who entered.

"Yes, Nikita?"

"A call from the airport. The jet has taken off and should arrive in Baku in several hours."

"We should be present when the money changes hands. Just to make sure it is our hands that receive it," the ex-KGB general commented.

The young man turned to leave. "I'll arrange for another plane," he called over his shoulder as he walked to the door.

A voice crackled through the shortwave speakers. "I see them in the distance," the pilot said.

"Use everything you've got aboard to eliminate them."

"It is like shooting wolves from the air," the voice bragged.

Donielev grinned. He glanced at the three sealed cases, filled with American currency. As he walked to them, he knew he needed to take another look at the American hundred dollar bills.

Opening the lids, he glanced at the stacks of fresh money and beamed. Then reluctantly he shut and locked the cases.

Soon it would all be his to spend.

"DO YOU KNOW how to get to the airport from here?"

"I think so," Tolstoy replied, struggling to keep control of the huge wheel.

Bolan heard the faint rotor throbs coming from the direction of the city.

A helicopter.

"We're getting company," he shouted over the roar of the truck engine.

She glanced in the sky and saw the approaching chopper. "Donielev," she replied loudly. "One of his own men, or some money-hungry mercenary he's paid."

"Let's not make it easy for them."

Tolstoy nodded. She twisted the wheel and pulled the truck from the roadway.

The ZIL 6x6 bumped its way across the open field, away from the cluster of trees. When the vehicle reached a wide dirt road, Tolstoy turned the wheel sharply and accelerated.

The helicopter closed the distance to overfly the moving truck, banking around to hover about sixty yards overhead, and continued to track the vehicle for several minutes.

Bolan knew that the pilot would take some sort of action soon unless the Executioner seized the initiative. He twisted his body into a low crouch as he swung the mounted machine gun around and up, tracking on the chopper.

The helicopter was practically on top of them, the throbbing of its rotors causing him to blink rapidly.

He saw one of the crew aboard the chopper leaning well out from the aircraft as the pilot maintained his holding position above and just off to the truck's left. There was a submachine gun in the man's hand. Bolan could see the muzzle-flashes as the gunner fired in his direction.

Tolstoy had seen the same movement and had kept the vehicle moving evasively.

None of the lead made contact—except with the ground.

Bolan registered one split-second impression of horrified expressions inside the chopper, the pilot and gunner reacting when they saw his quick turning of the mounted machine gun. The pilot worked his stick into an evasive maneuver. The aircraft wobbled slightly and started to bank up and away.

But it was too late.

Bolan opened fire, the weapon's reports piercing through the racket of the helicopter's rotors. The Executioner's body vibrated from the recoil as he rode a long, concentrated hail of fire. The gunship tilted and avoided the first wave of bullets.

The machine gunner reappeared, now holding a rocket launcher against his shoulder. Bolan recognized it as the Russian-made RPG-16, loaded with an armor-piercing warhead.

The Executioner had to get the helicopter before the rocket got them.

The gunship took the next murderous fusillade from close enough range to riddle the fuel tanks and rotor mechanism. The aircraft disintegrated into an eye-searing fireball that competed with the sun for brightness.

The explosion was forceful enough to almost shove the racing ZIL off the road. Bolan gripped the gun mount, bracing his wide-legged stance against the truck bed as he dodged flaming debris from the exploding chopper.

Inside the cab Tolstoy fought the wheel to maintain the truck's balance as she shifted, increasing the speed with the skill of a professional driver handling a runaway rig.

The charred debris that was the helicopter rained into a nearby wooded area, starting myriad brushfires.

While the colonel tried to regain full control of the truck, Bolan swung his machine gun on its mount. He saw no signs of any other approaching gunships.

There could be more on the way, but for now the sky was only filled with sunshine.

The soldier abandoned the machine gun and worked his way over the side of the truck bed, then eased himself through the open passenger window.

Tolstoy concentrated on the road ahead, then, without turning her head, said, "Somebody will come looking for the helicopter and this truck. Will they be waiting at the airport?"

"We'll be ready for them," he promised. "You worry about finding the scientists in Baku."

"I know someone who lives in the Azerbaijani city. I can call him for assistance."

Bolan was curious. "A friend?"

"My former brother-in-law. Rasul Aliyev. He's with the Azerbaijan Federal Police."

The soldier made an assumption. "You stayed friends after the divorce?"

"They're not divorced," Tolstoy said in a matter-of-fact voice. "She's dead."

Bolan could hear the pain in the woman's voice.

"She worked for the same KGB directorate as I did, protecting nuclear secrets. A team of agents from the Second Directorate accused her of attempting to sell our secrets to foreign powers." She paused, then added, "It was Donielev's way of getting even with me for not going to bed with him."

The outline of the airport was becoming visible in the distance. The colonel stopped the truck at the side of the road and turned to Bolan.

"You're going after him, aren't you?"

The soldier nodded.

"I would like to join you," she pleaded.

"One of us needs to catch up with Haverford. You've got the contacts," he replied.

"How will you know where to find Donielev?"

He would call the embassy from the airport. Knowing Brognola, there would be an address waiting for him with the embassy contact, Jim Hayslip.

"I'll know."

"And if Donielev left men behind at the airport?"

"The two of us will take care of them."

She smiled sadly. "Be careful. I need you."

As if she suddenly realized she had exposed her personal feelings, the woman added, "The world needs you to find the scientists and their plutonium before some madman can force them to make a nuclear bomb.''

Blinking the tears from her eyes, she quickly turned back to the wheel and started the truck in motion.

''I will make arrangements for a plane and pilot to be available to take you to Baku whenever you finish your business here,'' she said, suddenly all professional.

Bolan didn't answer. He was already developing a battle strategy that could only end in death—Donielev's, with any luck.

19

The dacha was exactly where Brognola said it would be, along the Rublyovskoy Shosse, an hour from Vnukovo Airport.

The head Fed had been thorough. The gray-haired embassy contact had arrived at the airport with a canvas bag filled with replacements for Bolan's depleted supplies, as well as his suitcase, retrieved from Irina Tolstoy's apartment. Using his credit card, Jim Hayslip rented a car for the Executioner, letting him select the vehicle he preferred.

The soldier chose a BMW 740 white sedan. The large German engine could generate enough power to push the vehicle to speeds of more than ninety miles per hour without causing the car to drift.

As the two men shook hands, the embassy representative wished Bolan luck.

He parked the BMW along a side wall of the dacha, then checked his weapons. The silenced Beretta, with a full magazine, was snug in its shoulder harness, a suppressed Uzi subgun had been slung over a shoulder and the Applegate-Fairbairn blade was sheathed in leather against his right leg.

He buckled the battle harness he extracted from the canvas bag around his waist and clipped on a pair of M-67 grenades. Extra clips for his weapons were slipped into the pouches of the belt. The Executioner was rigged for war.

THROUGH THE GAP between the wooden gate of the compound and the stone wall on which it was mounted, the Executioner saw the guard carefully studying the area in front of him.

The one thing Bolan knew for sure—hardmen, like rats, never ran alone. Where there was one, there were more.

The problem was that the soldier didn't know if the others were hiding outside or were inside the brick building.

The man was mafia, albeit Russian mafia. There was no mistaking the bulge of holstered hardware beneath the right arm. There was no mistaking the type. He was in his early twenties, but had the eyes of stone killer.

It was time to go into action. The soldier pushed open the wooden gate and deliberately stepped into view. He held his Beretta against his right leg, where it wasn't easily visible.

The guard spotted him at once. His reaction was swift and it sealed his fate. The Skorpion SMG that swung up and at Bolan told the Executioner everything he needed to know. The man was guarding something—or someone—important. That someone could only be Donielev.

Bolan extended the Beretta 93-R to arm's length and stroked the trigger, firing a single shot that cored a hole through the sentry's brain. The body slumped against the side of the building, then slid to the ground, brushing a path of blood on its journey downward.

The Executioner listened at the door for sounds of movement inside. There weren't any. He tried the doorknob, which turned, and the door swung partway open. He listened for a moment, then shoved it open all the way. A wide man with a badly botched crew cut tumbled backward into the inside front hall, losing his balance and falling to the floor. A second shadowy figure was behind him, and he rushed at Bolan.

Two more men kicked a rear door open and rushed into the room, Skorpion SMGs up and ready. The first hardman started to get to his feet.

Grasping his attacker's wrist, Bolan used the man's own momentum to send him crashing into the gunner behind him, then he spun in one fluid movement to fend off the frontal assault by the other two. His right foot continued lifting in a high arc. The kick connected with the nearer thug's rib cage, snapping bone as the would-be killer was driven back against the door frame.

The second hood tried to jump on the Executioner's back and pull him to the floor. But Bolan let his fury concentrate in the edge of his right palm as he slashed it against his assailant's carotid artery. With only a small "whoosh" to signal his death, the mafia soldier fell backwards against his partner.

Casting his dead friend aside, the guy with the crew cut reached for a long-bladed knife he'd hidden in his waist band. Then rushed at the Executioner, screeching a curse as he held the blade in the air.

Bolan let him get closer, then stepped aside and twisted the man's knife hand. Struggling, the mafia tough tried to twist his hand free from his adversary's grip. As he strained, concentrating every ounce of his nearly three hundred pounds in his effort to pull away, the hood broke out in a sweat. Veins popped out on both sides of his head, seeming ready to burst.

Bolan let the tough's strength do the majority of the work, just making sure the blade didn't come any closer.

Finally the hardman gasped for air, then began to resume the battle. To his horror, the hand that held the razor sharp blade refused to do his bidding. Inch by inch, it started pushing back to his face, guided there by the American's hand.

He knew he had to break away, but the American wouldn't let him go. He felt the blade touch his jacket, then pierce it and his shirt. With one last, desperate effort, he used both hands to push the man away, then felt the blade slice beneath his skin and through his ribs.

The Executioner let the man slide to the floor, where blood leaked from the wound and pooled under the corpse.

A man appeared at the front door, clutching a 9 mm Makarov pistol in his left hand. He started to call out names. "Miki. Leon. Oleg. Georgi. Where are you? Somebody shot Dimitri."

He stopped talking when he saw the bodies of the four men on the floor. When he looked up and stared at the cold face of the man who'd killed them, he snap-aimed his pistol in an attempt to forestall the inevitable. But it was too late.

The blade that Bolan had thrown at his neck had already bitten into his throat.

YURI DONIELEV SAT in his living room, totally immersed in the loud music that poured from the stereo speakers. He couldn't keep his eyes from straying back to the three metal money containers.

Finally he had packed everything he wanted to carry on the plane to Baku or have shipped to the storage company he had called in Rome. Many of the objects he had spent years collecting would have to be left behind. But his former mentor, in a rare moment of kindness, had responded to his telephone call and agreed to sell his properties and art objects for him. The money would be deposited in one of Donielev's bank accounts in Zurich, Khreshchatik promised.

For some reason, Donielev believed the man. He had no choice. There wasn't enough time for him to handle the sales himself.

At least, he thought, smiling, he would have the things he loved most with him: the money from the Russian government and, later tonight, the money from the Iranians.

He checked his wristwatch. The truck picking up the possessions to be carried on the plane was already ten minutes late. As soon as it arrived and he supervised the loading, he and the dozen guards would leave for the airport.

He stared at the metal boxes again. He had taken samples from each case and had them checked at the banks. They weren't counterfeit.

Donielev had fifteen million dollars in American hundred-dollar bills. A fortune, even for a millionaire like himself.

The temptation was too great. He had opened and closed the lids several times, but he had to have another quick look at all the money before he had them loaded on the plane.

Pulling himself up from the easy chair, he walked to the containers and stroked each as if it were a beautiful woman he was caressing, then opened the lids. Donielev stared at the vast amount of American currency and felt like Aladdin. Only his magic lamp could be spent.

Reaching into the cases, he grabbed wrapped stacks of hundred-dollar bills and pressed them to his chest, to his face. He had never felt so happy. All this money was his to enjoy, and he wouldn't share it with anyone.

Then Donielev smelled something burning, the rank aroma of charring flesh. He looked down and saw flames in his hands. His shirt was on fire. He touched his face and jumped from the pain.

The ex-KGB general threw the burning money to the floor. His prized antique Persian rug absorbing the flames.

A tower of fire began to rise from each of the metal cases. Ignoring the pain from the burns to his hands, his chest, his face, Donielev ran to the containers and tried to put out the flames.

He had been cheated by the Americans, by his own government. Insane with agony, he shouted that he would get even.

There was a gun on the sideboard, a 5.45 mm PSM autoloader. Donielev grabbed it and ran to the door to kill the enemies he knew had to be nearby.

THE EXECUTIONER headed toward the next door along the corridor, checking left and right to make sure no gunmen lay in wait. He had systematically done a room-by-room search, and so far hadn't found Donielev.

The door opened suddenly, and a nightmare figure that vaguely resembled Yuri Donielev stumbled into the corridor. His face and upper body were charred, as if someone had set a torch to him.

Behind the scorched figure, Bolan could see flames shooting up from metal cases. As he looked back at the horror in front of him, he knew Brognola's plan had worked.

Extremely well.

The phosphorous compound had absorbed enough oxygen to burst into flames.

"I know you!" Donielev roared as he stared at the Executioner. "You are the American. You tried to kill me!" He raised the autoloader.

"Death!" he screamed.

"You first," Bolan replied as he squeezed the Uzi's trigger.

Three 9 mm death seekers hit home, chewing into Donielev's chest. With a look of surprise on his face, the mafia chief fell back into the living room and slid to the floor.

Bolan knelt at his side. Forcing himself to lean close to the charred mask that covered the skull of the former KGB general, he asked a question.

"Where in Baku are the scientists?"

Donielev stared past the Executioner at some distant point. He would never answer Bolan's question. Not in this lifetime.

The soldier got to his feet and turned to leave. He could hear the sounds of a truck outside. It wouldn't be wise to be found here, with all the bodies strewed around the compound.

Slipping out the back door, he worked his way to where he had parked the BMW. Dropping the Uzi on the seat beside him, Bolan started the engine and burned rubber as he headed for the airport and Baku.

20

Bina was finally visible from the small commercial jet. Irina Tolstoy studied the small international airport that fed the city of Baku. She checked in her handbag for her official passport. The Azeris were suspicious of all Russians visiting their country. The Tokarev she carried would have to be left on the plane.

She had called her former brother-in-law from the airport in Moscow before the jet took off. Rasul Aliyev had sounded pleased that she was coming to Azerbaijan.

"Can you meet me at the airport?"

"Of course, Irina. With pleasure," he promised. "But what is the occasion for this visit?"

Quickly she briefed him on the missing scientists and plutonium.

"I would be grateful for anything you can find out," she said, then added, "I should arrive in three hours."

AS THE PLANE taxied toward the terminal, the redheaded woman wondered where the scientists and their plutonium were being held. If not in Baku itself, someplace close by the city.

Without sources it would be hard to find them in a city with more than one and a half million inhabitants. And she suspected the Azeris would be less than cooperative.

Perhaps mentioning the Iranians would get their attention. Despite the fact that most of the Azeris were Muslims, they had no love for their neighbors across the Caspian Sea.

Tolstoy knew a lot about Azerbaijan and its people. Her own sister had married one of them. For one thing, she knew that the Azeris believed in making money, while the Iranians believed in making war. To the people of Azerbaijan, the only good thing about the government of Iran was that it kept its revolution on its own side of the vast inland sea that made them neighbors.

Because she had gained a personal interest in the subject since Tamara married Rasul, Tolstoy had done a great deal of research on the country.

Its capital, Baku, sat on a virtual sea of oil. For many centuries the city had been a prize fought for by opposing armies. Rivaled only by the reserves in Iran, Baku had enough crude oil to fuel the world for many years.

Even ancient visitors had been impressed by the "Towers of Fire" that had sprung from the grounds around the area. Flames, fed by natural-gas springs and oil, shot into the air, giving the region a look more identified by the superstitious with Hades than with this world, and had awed all who had passed through the land.

As if that wasn't enough, Azerbaijan itself had a wealth of rich soil, capable of growing cereals, cotton, grapes and a multitude of other crops.

Yet the country—and its capital—had fallen on hard times. The ethnic battles with the Armenians, who were their hated neighbors, had drained the treasury's coffers. Foreign oil companies were reluctant to invest desperately needed funds until the conflict was resolved.

The dissolution of the Soviet Union had forced the Azeris to use a large portion of their treasury rebuilding their military forces. Equipment was scarce and expensive.

If the Russians didn't occasionally donate some of their surplus equipment, many Azeri soldiers were certain that they would have to use rocks and wooden clubs as weapons, and bicycles as vehicles.

The colonel knew that, like everywhere else in the former Soviet republics, corruption was rampant. Bribes were expected for the slightest favor. Salaries didn't cover the cost of surviving, so that even the most powerful government officials expected payment for their assistance.

THE TALL MAN who waited on the other side of the customs barrier beamed as he saw Tolstoy walk toward him. He wrapped his huge arms around her and squeezed until she had to push him away.

Gasping for air, she asked, "Has it been that long, Rasul?"

"A lifetime, my darling Irina. Your niece and nephew are about to graduate from their universities, and yet you look as young as you did when they were only infants," Aliyév commented.

"No wonder Tamara loved you so much," Tolstoy said with admiration. "What woman could resist such compliments?"

He looked embarrassed.

"I was sorry about what happened to Oleg," she said softly, referring to the murder of her nephew, Rasul's oldest child.

The police major looked sad. "A tragedy. He had called me the night before to tell me he had made some big deal and was planning to leave Moscow for a while."

He decided to change the subject and looked at her empty hand. "But where are your suitcases?"

"I didn't have time to pack."

Aliyev shrugged. "No matter. You can buy whatever you need in Baku. We are a big, modern city now." He led the way to where he had parked his vehicle, a relatively new Chaika.

Tolstoy stared at it. "You must have come into money, Rasul."

"No. Just a promotion." He looked proud. "You are now looking at *Major* Rasul Aliyev, of the Azerbaijan Federal Police."

She clapped her hands gleefully. "If only Tamara could be here to share your success."

Aliyev's face became solemn. "If that creature who murdered her were here today—"

She stopped him. "There is a man who is dedicated to making sure he does not do the same to anyone else ever again," she said gravely. "Which is why I have rushed here."

The Azeri police major helped Tolstoy into the car, then got behind the wheel and started the engine. "So you said on the telephone. Something about some nuclear scientists being flown here by kidnappers."

"Did you have a chance to find out when they arrived and where they went?"

He shook his head. "I have one lead, but it can wait until you get to visit with the children. They are coming to my house to eat supper with you."

"It can't wait, Rasul. As much as I love them, this must come first."

The Azeri major sighed. "At least you are carrying a weapon, aren't you?"

Tolstoy shook her head. "I didn't think I'd get past your customs with one. You know how the Azerbaijani government feels about Russians. But I was hoping you could provide me with one."

"Later," the major said. "You are sure you want to follow up on this lead first?"

"Positive," she insisted.

"Well, it's your decision to make," he said as he put the vehicle in gear and drove away from the airport.

WHILE WAITING at the airport for the Atomic Energy Ministry jet, Bolan placed a call to Brognola at his hotel, finally tracking him down at the American Embassy.

"I just heard the news about Donielev," the head Fed said. "How does that affect your search?"

"Haverford took the men and flew to Baku. The colonel went ahead to find out anything she could. Her former brother-in-law is a senior cop in Azerbaijan," Bolan reported.

"Maybe he's still one of the good guys," Brognola commented, sounding cynical. "When you get there, contact a woman named Seppi Lawrence at the embassy. She doesn't know anything about you except that you're on special assignment for the White House."

"Agency operative?"

"Not important. She's got her own agenda and it's not pro-Iran."

Brognola changed the subject. "The Man called me a little while ago. If you find the two scientists and they want to move to the United States, don't discourage them. The presidential elections are coming up soon."

Bolan didn't like what he was hearing. Rescuing the two from Haverford and the Iranians was one thing. Convincing them to defect was never part of the mission.

He told the Stony Man Farm chief that.

"The CIA is more than willing to handle that last part," Brognola commented, then added, "Ask Seppi Lawrence for anything you need. Take care."

After a brief goodbye, Bolan broke the connection.

HAVERFORD HAD mixed feelings about the death of Yuri Donielev. The newspapers and television news programs reported that the former KGB major-general and his bodyguards had been killed by home invaders.

Several had speculated that Donielev had been involved in some criminal activities since his dismissal from the KGB.

But there was no positive evidence, according to the reporters.

Much of what the dead ex-KGB general had handled was now Haverford's responsibility, such as paying off the local authorities, especially the police. Luckily he had brought along one of his staff, Gilal Kurbanov, to handle the locals.

He had to make a decision about what he wanted done when the police major who was on Donielev's payroll had called earlier to warn him that someone from Moscow was arriving in Baku to hunt for some missing nuclear specialists.

If that wasn't enough to cope with, several fights had already broken out between different members of the gang about who would take over leadership now that Donielev was dead. Haverford knew the battles for leadership wouldn't end until one of the gang members was declared chief.

It was time for him to leave. With Donielev dead, there was no reason to stay in Azerbaijan or in Russia.

He had only one thing left to do, then he could fly back to Washington, D.C., and take some time off from business.

After he delivered the two scientists and their ''luggage'' to the Iranians and accepted the agreed-upon payment in hard currency, he would fly back to Moscow, pay his staff in advance for three months to keep their loyalty, then continue on to the United States.

He had spoken to Yaneri, his Iranian contact. The delivery was due the following day. The Iranians had agreed to make the exchange in Buzovna, a small coastal village near Baku, then transport the two scientists on one of their high-speed power cruisers across the Caspian Sea to Iran.

It was important to keep Donielev's men from killing one another, at least until the Iranians left.

Haverford drew his 9 mm Smith & Wesson Model 59 and stepped in the middle of the living room. He called out an order in fluent Russian. "As long as I'm alive, I'm the leader of this group."

He glared at the two dozen men crowded into the small room. "Anybody disagree?"

He could see several of the men working their fingers toward holstered pistols. One touched the leather of the holster mounted on his belt. Haverford fired at the itchy hand, and the man screamed with pain as the lead slug tore through his palm.

The others looked at their comrade and placed their hands on their laps where the ex-CIA agent could see them.

Haverford turned to one of the men, a small, slim man with squinting eyes. "There should be antiseptic in the medicine kit we brought. Pour some on the wound and bandage his hand," he ordered.

He led the wounded man to the kitchen where the medical kit was.

Haverford repeated his question. "Anybody here disagree with what I said?"

The living room was filled with total silence.

"Good. Tomorrow morning the Iranians arrive to take charge of the two men upstairs." He had locked the nuclear scientists and their plutonium in one of the small bedrooms on the upper floor.

"Until then, I want at least six men guarding the outside and inside of this house."

Haverford walked up the stairs. Already he was working on a plan to rid himself of his partners. Thirty million dollars was better shared by one person than by twenty-one.

"TELL ME ABOUT where we are going," Irina Tolstoy said.

Her former brother-in-law seemed nervous as he drove into the city, then turned onto one of the main thoroughfares and headed into the foothills overlooking the large seaport.

"All I know is that someone told me this farmhouse in the foothills had been rented to foreigners for a week. One of the neighbors, an old woman, noticed several dozen men move in and never come out again. The men, she told one of my officers, looked like criminals." He smiled. "But everybody looks like a criminal to an elderly widow who lives alone."

He pointed to a small wooden structure set back behind a stand of trees. "That's the house."

"Pull up to the door, then come with me," Tolstoy said.

They both got out of the vehicle and walked to the front door. Before either had a chance to knock, the front door swung open. A tall, stately-looking older man smiled at the major, then saw the redheaded woman.

In fluent Russian he said, "Come in, Colonel. We've been waiting for you."

She started to turn and run, then saw the Smith & Wesson Model 59 in his hand. The tall man turned to the major. "You can leave now. We'll take care of her."

Stunned, Tolstoy stared at her former brother-in-law. Looking embarrassed, he kept his gaze lowered.

"A policeman cannot send his children to the universities on what he is paid. I'm sorry, Irina."

Then he walked back to his car as Haverford pulled her into the house.

21

Bolan was worried. Tolstoy hadn't left a message for him at the American Embassy. Then he remembered her former brother-in-law.

He called the Azerbaijan Federal Police headquarters and asked for Rasul Aliyev.

"Major Aliyev is out on a call. May I take a message?"

The soldier hung up without replying. He looked around the borrowed office for a telephone book.

The conservatively dressed young woman sitting behind the desk, an assistant commercial attaché, asked if she could help him. The Executioner wondered if she was CIA. Brognola had given him her name as the embassy contact. Seppi Lawrence. An unusual name.

She was attractive. Her dark brown hair was cut short, which made her large brown eyes look even larger. Bolan guessed that she was in her early thirties.

"Do you have a local telephone directory?"

She opened the bottom drawer of her desk and fished out a large book.

When Bolan opened it, he realized the language was different than anything he had ever seen before.

The woman watching him smiled.

"It's Azeri-Turkic, Mr. Belasko. A variation of the Turkish language."

He looked frustrated. "And one I can't read."

She looked at the tall man. He was impressive looking. She wondered if he was with one of the many American oil companies bidding for drilling rights in Azerbaijan. If that was all he was, why would someone who held the rank of presidential adviser, like Harold Brognola, have instructed the ambassador to provide him with any assistance he requested? No, he had to be more than that. But what? She set aside her questions and smiled at him.

"But I can. Who are you looking for?"

He looked at her with gratitude. "See if there is a listing for a Rasul Aliyev."

She thought for a moment. "I've heard that name before. Isn't he with the federal police?"

"Yes."

She studied the American again and wondered why he wanted to call an Azeri policeman at home. She searched the list of names until she came to the right one, then scribbled the number on a small pad.

Handing it over, she asked, "Would you like me to dial it for you? You might get a little flustered if someone answered in the local dialect."

"Thank you. Where'd you learn to speak Azeri-Turkic?"

"At home, in Los Angeles. There are more than a hundred thousand Azeris living in California. A third of our neighbors back home had emigrated from Azerbaijan. So in my case, it was learn the language or give up going to a lot of birthday and sleepover parties."

"From your first name I would have thought you were of Azerbaijan descent."

"Actually 'Seppi' is Iranian. My father was with the late Shah's government before the revolution. He escaped to the United States, met my mother there and married her."

"'Lawrence' isn't an Iranian name," Bolan commented.

"He took my mother's maiden name to avoid being bothered by members of the Shah's secret police who were searching the United States for anyone they could blackmail."

"I remember the Shah's secret police. A snake pit of cold-blooded killers," he said. "Their successors, the VEVAK, aren't any better."

"Worse because they've been more successful at killing anybody who doesn't agree with their government's policies."

Dialing the number as she spoke, the young embassy clerk waited for someone to answer, then spoke rapidly into the phone.

"You've lucked out, Mr. Belasko. The woman on the other end speaks English."

She handed the phone to Bolan. "Holler if I can do anything else for you. Meantime I'll sign out a vehicle from the car pool for you."

She grinned at him, then vanished down the corridor.

Bolan put the phone to his ear. "I'm trying to reach Colonel Irina Tolstoy," he said.

"This is her niece. My aunt had to rush back to Moscow on some government emergency." She paused, then added, "My brother and I never even got to see her before she had to leave."

Something was wrong. Brognola would have left a message at the embassy if a crisis had arisen.

"How do you know she had to leave?"

"My father drove her back to the airport last night, before we even got home from school."

"Do you know where I can reach your father?"

"No. But he usually comes home for dinner, even if he has to go out on assignment later. He should be here by six tonight. Can I tell him who called him?"

"I'll reach him later," Bolan said, and hung up.

He wandered down the corridor and found Lawrence in another office. Looking up from a desk full of paperwork, she smiled at him.

"There's a vehicle waiting for you. A Jeep Cherokee, if that's all right."

"That should work."

The woman handed him a business card. Printed on the front was the seal of the United States, the address and the telephone number of the embassy.

"My home number is on the back. Call me if I can be helpful." He sensed that the invitation was only partially professional.

"I wonder if I can get you to make another call for me?"

She opened her drawer and took out a Baku phone book. "Sure. To whom?"

"Can you call the airport and check with the airlines if a Colonel Irina Tolstoy departed for Moscow sometime today?"

The young woman thought for a moment. "I can try. There are only a few airlines flying from Baku to Moscow. The local Azeri-owned line, Azal Airlines, and the Aeroflot domestic affiliate. Of course, there are others she could have taken but she would have gone through Ankara or Tbilisi before heading for Moscow."

She dialed the first number and spoke softly into the phone, then waited.

A voice on the other end came back on the line. The young woman said a few words and hung up.

"She wasn't listed as a passenger on the Azeri airline," she reported as she dialed another number.

"The Russian airline can sometimes be less cooperative," she warned.

"Tell them she is a senior official of the Russian Federation Ministry of Atomic Energy," Bolan suggested.

"I can try," she commented, then spoke rapidly in fluent Russian.

This time Bolan understood her question.

"Did a Colonel Irina Tolstoy, of the Russian Federation Ministry of Atomic Energy, take a flight back to Moscow today?"

She waited until the male voice on the other end returned. This time the soldier could hear the reply. *Nyet.* No.

Lawrence hung up the phone and asked a question. "Sorry. Was she important to you?"

She turned to see the massively built American's reaction, but he was gone.

MASSOUD YANERI HAD requisitioned the large house usually occupied by the Iranian ambassador to Azerbaijan. Located just off Nizami Square, the ancient structure sheltered more than thirty members of the Iranian Revolutionary Guards and three dozen agents and technicians from the Ministry of Intelligence.

A network of communications equipment filled half the large basement and allowed the Iranian embassy direct contact with government offices in Tehran. A second network, consisting of sophisticated eavesdropping equipment, permitted staffers around-the-clock access to confidential conversations in most of the Azerbaijan government offices. In addition, bribes to key technical personnel in the government telephone-equipment headquarters gave the Iranians access to every telephone in the country, including those connecting the embassies of foreign countries with their governments. Only the handful of embassies with telephone-scrambling devices, like the United States, were safe from the constant monitoring of their calls.

Sometimes he wondered how the Azeris would react if those his government hadn't bribed knew about the taps. But like any intelligent Iranian government official, Yaneri was positive that it was his right to listen in on any conversation taking place in Azerbaijan. After all, hadn't the Persians owned the country a thousand years before there was a Soviet Union?

The oil that bubbled in vast quantities under the Apsheron Peninsula, on which Baku was located, and the oil trying to force its way up from underneath the Caspian Sea rightfully belonged to Iran.

As did Azerbaijan.

Someday, Yaneri was positive, Iran would be able to reclaim this cursed land.

One of the telephones Yaneri had ordered monitored was the one that led from the house Haverford had rented.

The technician that brought the deputy minister of Intelligence the tape of telephone calls from Haverford's safehouse offered a comment. "There are two calls made to the house in the last two hours—and one from the house—that may interest you, Mr. Minister."

The Iranian deputy Intelligence minister looked at the antique clock on the desk. He had two hours before he was supposed to have a preliminary meeting with the American to establish final arrangements for the exchange of the scientists and their fuel for his country's money. Instead he hoped to convince the former CIA spy-master to make the trade at no expense to his government. And in exchange, continue to stay alive. The choice would be the American's.

Yaneri waited for the specialist to leave, then dropped the tape into a player. Leaning back in the ambassador's chair, he stroked his long, silky mustache, pressed the Play button and listened.

Both of the incoming calls were for the American who was to deliver the nuclear scientists in the morning. The first was from an Azeri police major.

"This is Major Aliyev. Somebody called my home and asked for Colonel Tolstoy. When my daughter told the caller she had been called back to Moscow, he asked how he could reach me. He has my address. What should I tell him if he comes here?''

Yaneri recognized the second voice. Haverford.

"Calm down. Bring him here and we'll handle the rest."

The second call was from someone with a Farsi accent. At first Yaneri thought it had been placed by an Iranian traitor.

"Mr. Haverford. I am with my uncle. He has agreed to lend us his farmhouse. I also called a friend, a helicopter pilot with the local military forces. He will make himself available for the right amount of money."

"Agree to whatever he wants. Just have him meet us here within the hour. He can land behind the house."

Yaneri pressed his lips together and tried to analyze the two calls.

Haverford had already put the two scientists on a helicopter. Or was about to do so. But to go where?

The Iranian stopped the tape and lifted a phone. He dialed an internal number and asked one of the specialists to come into the office.

A few minutes later the door opened, and a thin, quiet man with piercing eyes entered.

"Mohammed, can you determine a telephone number from the dial sounds?"

"If they are not distorted, Mr. Minister."

"How can we find out where that telephone is located?"

The man smiled. "We have friends in the Azerbaijan telephone headquarters."

Yaneri had one more call he wanted to hear—the outgoing one the technician had mentioned.

"Come back in ten minutes and pick up the tape." He leaned across the desk and stared coldly at the Intelligence analyst. "But I will need that address within an hour from the time you start listening."

He turned his back on the man and pressed the Play button.

The voice was that of a woman. She was whispering, and it sounded as if she were in pain.

"Maryam? This is Irina, your aunt. Please listen. If anyone calls and asks for me, please give him this address." She gave the location of Haverford's safehouse. "If no one calls in the next hour, please contact the American Embassy and leave my name and this location for a Mr. Michael Belasko. And, Maryam, please don't tell your father I called."

As the female voice gave directions to the woman on the other end of the line, Yaneri wondered who the woman was and why she was in the house that Haverford was using. The other name, Michael Belasko, sounded familiar. He would have to check it out when he had more time.

22

Staying in the shadows, Mack Bolan moved toward the farmhouse in the foothills of Baku. The Jeep Cherokee was parked nearby, behind some trees.

The Executioner's face was covered with combat cosmetics, making his detection more difficult.

A slight hot breeze brushed across his booted ankles as he trotted to the building. Before Bolan could reach the target, however, automatic-weapons fire began eating up the ground around him. Random strays were coming in with sudden accuracy, and the soldier whipped around to find a pair of mafia hardmen bearing down on him.

He unslung the suppressed Uzi and washed away the lives of both street soldiers with a burning wave of 9 mm death.

The Executioner checked both fallen gunmen to make sure neither was faking it, then, satisfied they were dead, he moved closer to the wooden building.

He could hear loud music and see lights burning in the rear of the structure as he moved into the house, past the foyer and into the darkened living room. In silence he followed the source of illumination.

Risking a glimpse around the door frame, he glimpsed three men sitting around a table, playing cards. Scanning the room, Bolan saw no one who looked like a research-institute professor, or bulky canisters that could contain plutonium.

The men were cursing in a thick dialect that identified them as coming from one of the former Soviet republics south of Russia. Bolan had difficulty translating the words.

The nearest hardman asked, "You hear that noise outside, Nikki?"

The bald man facing him shrugged. "Probably one of those Azeri cowboys the American hired getting in some target practice on a rat."

"Good thing they don't get to share in the pot. The American must have brought in a dozen or more gunmen," the third man at the table commented as he stood and walked to the refrigerator. He took out a liter of bottled mineral water. Tilting the bottle to his lips, he took a long swallow.

"Hey, that's for all of us, Mikhail!"

"We've got a whole case of the stuff," the third hardman snapped, intervening.

Then he turned to Mikhail. "Too bad about the guys we had to bury back in Moscow."

"Everybody's got to die sometime," he replied cynically. "Like the woman upstairs. I'd like another crack at her before we have to put her to sleep."

"Maybe after the American gets back from dealing with the Iranians." Then Nikki added, "I wonder why he didn't have a quick one before he took off?"

"Who knows? Maybe he likes boys."

Mikhail looked surprised. "You really think the American's a homosexual?"

"I don't know and I don't care. All I care about is getting paid and getting out of this hick country."

"Where did he and all those mercenaries he hired go?"

"Who cares?"

"He said in case there was trouble, we were to contact this guy Gilal and tell him."

Nikki glanced at the refrigerator. "Isn't that the number of where he's staying?"

Mikhail nodded, then asked, "Do you think we ought to go upstairs and check on the redhead?"

"You've done that twice already. Boy, you are a hog where women are concerned. Besides, she isn't going anywhere."

"Yeah, but you are. Your turn to relieve Vladimir."

"Shit. It's boring out there. And I really hate these Azeri cowboys."

"Outside." The word was snapped by the man who apparently was in charge. "You'll be relieved in an hour."

Bolan had heard enough. He stepped through the doorway, his Beretta unleathered and extended in a two-handed grip. The man the others had called Nikki saw him and grabbed for the 9 mm Mauser tucked into his waistband.

The Beretta coughed twice. The 9 mm rounds punched holes in Nikki's throat, tearing open his carotid artery, and raced out the other side.

As the corpse fell forward, the surviving hardmen dived to the floor, drawing their pistols. Bolan made a half turn and drilled a triburst into the stomach of the nearer hardman, then pointed the Beretta at the third man, who'd taken cover under the table.

"On your feet," the soldier snapped in Russian.

As the hardman crawled out and started to get up, his hand slid to the Tokarev pistol inside his waistband. Bolan fired a single round, aiming carefully so it tore a clean hole through the guy's palm.

"You'll live," Bolan promised, "if you start talking."

"I don't know anything," the man growled, clutching his shattered palm with his other hand as he fell into one of the chairs.

"Is the woman upstairs alive?"

"Yes. The American slammed her around a few times to get her to talk."

"Is that all that happened to her?"

The man kept looking at the blood spurting from the hole in his palm. "I need a doctor."

"Start talking or you'll need an undertaker. Is that all that happened to her?"

"Mikhail," the wounded street soldier replied with hesitation, looking at one of the bodies, "went upstairs to see her a couple of times."

The hardman was taken aback by the look on Bolan's face.

"But I didn't know what he had in mind. I really didn't!"

"Where are the scientists?"

"The American put them on a helicopter." He looked at his shattered hand. "Please, I need a doctor."

"Where?"

"The American didn't tell me."

Bolan pressed the Beretta against the man's temple. "That's a shame."

"No," the man begged. "He really didn't. He's got a man with him who was going to hide them at his uncle's place. That's all I know."

"Where is the American?"

"He went to a meeting with some Iranians," the man said through gritted teeth, trying to fight the pain he was feeling. "Please, I'm bleeding."

"Where's the meeting?"

The man started to deny that he knew, then looked at the ice in Bolan's eyes. Changing his mind, he replied, "The American was asked to go to the Iranian embassy. When he refused, he suggested another place. Some old warehouse on Zorge Street that the man who works for him knew about. I heard him giving the Iranians directions."

"How many men did he take with him?"

"I don't—"

A single shot rang out from behind Bolan and punched into the mafia mobster's face. As he fell forward, the soldier spun, ready to trigger a round.

Then he saw Tolstoy. Her face and chest were badly beaten. She seemed unaware that she was naked from the waist up.

Her eyes, filled with shame, told the whole story. She had to have freed herself from the ropes that bound her and found a 9 mm Walther PPK someplace in the house.

Bolan tore the tablecloth from the kitchen table and handed it to Irina.

She ignored the offer, kneeling and unbuttoning the bloodied shirt on the corpse at her feet. Pulling it from the still-bleeding body, she slipped her hands into the sleeves, rolled them up and buttoned the shirt, then tied the bottom of the shirt around her waist. She knelt again and relieved the dead thug of his Tokarev pistol. A quick search of his pockets yielded three full clips.

Staring at the body of the hardman she'd just killed, she said, "He came upstairs after the first one was finished."

Her voice was filled with hate.

HAL BROGNOLA PACKED his suitcase, muttering to himself as he did. Bolan hadn't contacted him for almost a full day, so he had no idea how close he was to liberating the missing scientists.

That was what he'd had to tell the President earlier in the day.

"I'm not trying to put pressure on you, Hal," the Man had said, "but I've had a call from the director of the CIA. He told me Striker is raising hell. He's been there less than three days and he's already filled the morgues of two Moscow hospitals."

Brognola tried to reason with his superior. "It was in self-defense. And the men who'd been killed were all members of the mafia."

"The young woman who was murdered. You know, the one who worked for the Atomic Energy Ministry. Was she in the mafia?"

"First of all, we don't know that Striker had anything to do with her death. Besides, the dead woman's lover was one of the top brass in the KGB before it closed shop and runs one of the major mafia gangs in Moscow."

"I need results, Hal," the President said pointedly. "And I need them fast. The CIA's offered to send in a dozen of their best field agents to wrap up the search for the scientists and the plutonium."

"Don't make a decision until I get back. My flight gets into New York early tomorrow. I can grab the shuttle and be in your office before five."

The voice on the other end of the scrambled phone sighed. "Okay. I can wait that long before I have to decide."

After he hung up, Brognola placed a call to Seppi Lawrence at the American Embassy in Baku. All she could tell him was that Michael Belasko had come in and checked for messages and had borrowed a car from the embassy pool. He had called later to see if anyone had tried to reach him, but she had no information about where Belasko was staying or where he could be reached.

Brognola hoped the Executioner was getting close to wrapping up the mission. Otherwise he knew the President would release the hunt dogs.

And Mack Bolan just might get in their way.

23

Bolan and Tolstoy knelt behind a stand of trees and studied the warehouse. Three police vehicles were parked at the side of the road: a pair of Chaikas were parked in the driveway of the factory building, and next to them a ZIL limousine.

They watched as a pair of Jeeps, bearing the official insignia of the Iran government on their doors, pulled up to the warehouse and parked on the empty street. Six men in combat uniforms got out of the vehicles. Five of them, armed with snub-nose Uzi pistols, surrounded the sixth man and escorted him into the building.

The Executioner had seen photographs of the surrounded Iranian—Massoud Yaneri, deputy minister of Intelligence for Iran.

He leaned over and whispered, "This may be where the swap takes place."

Tolstoy nodded, keeping her eyes and weapon focused on the front door of the warehouse.

"I'll be right back," he said. "I want to see who's inside."

A pair of uniformed policemen stood in front of the warehouse, smoking cigarettes and chatting with a tall bald man who cradled a Skorpion SMG in his hands.

Bolan moved around to a side of the building and found a dirt-streaked window. He stood to one side and risked a peek inside.

Row after row of crates were stacked against a far wall. The markings were difficult to make out, but he finally realized what the wooden boxes contained—weapons and ammunition.

The warehouse was an arms depot. He suspected the crates had been hijacked from government storerooms and hidden in the warehouse to be sold to anyone who could afford the price.

There were more than a dozen men in the open area in front of the stacked boxes, most of them with the passionless expression of mafia street soldiers, mercenaries or members of the Iranian Revolutionary Guards.

He searched the room for the two scientists, but neither was visible.

The two men in the center got his attention. The tall, stately-looking man, wearing a conservative sports jacket, tan trousers and tasseled penny loafers, looked as stuffy as he had at the Moscow casino.

Maxwell Haverford.

The second man, the one the American was shaking hands with, was Massoud Yaneri.

The men were smiling at each other as they spoke.

If Bolan wanted to hear what they were saying, he would have to get inside the warehouse. Quickly he rejoined Tolstoy.

"Haverford and Yaneri are in there," he whispered, "but there's no sign of the scientists."

"Was there a tall, dark-skinned man wearing a police major's uniform with them?"

"Yeah, there was."

"We must get inside," she insisted, "so we can interrogate the American and the Iranian."

He glanced at the expression on the woman's face and wondered if they both had the same agenda.

"Wait here. I'll be right back."

Slipping away from Tolstoy's side, Bolan worked his way in the shadows to where he had parked the Jeep. Cautiously he opened the driver's door and eased himself inside. The canvas carryall was still on the floor where he'd left it. He opened it and searched through the contents, coming up with a grayish white block of plastic explosive.

Carefully he sliced the brick in two. Reaching into the bag again, he found a pair of detonators and pressed one into each of the plastic halves, then slipped out of the car and headed toward the building.

The side door he found was locked. Bolan wondered if it was wired with an alarm that went off when the door was opened.

Carefully inserting a thin lock pick and spreading its narrow steel tongs, he manipulated the device until the lock finally released its hold.

Bolan slowly moved the door inward, hoping it didn't open directly on the large area inside. He found himself in a smaller storeroom, filled with more wooden crates.

The contents were printed on the outside: 5.45 mm, 5.56 mm and 9 mm copper-jacketed ammunition; Russian rockets, launchers, AK-47s, a case of Makarov pistols.

Pressing one of the blocks of plastique against a crate, the Executioner set the timer for ten minutes, then moved past the stacks toward another doorway.

He risked a look around the corner and could see Haverford and Yaneri still talking, surrounded by armed men. No one bothered to glance in his direction, but he knew that someone would eventually.

He pressed the second brick of plastique against another case of rockets and set the timer.

It was time to get out of the building. Quickly retreating, he made his way out of the side door and back to Tolstoy's side.

"In five minutes anybody who's still alive will be running out of the front door," he warned.

"What about the missing scientists?"

A woman's voice behind them answered her question. "I think I can help you find them."

Bolan and Tolstoy turned toward the voice.

The Executioner recognized the woman—Seppi Lawrence.

She was wearing a pair of combat pants, as well as combat boots and jacket. Her brown hair was tucked under a military peaked cap.

"Sorry to take you by surprise, Mr. Belasko, but I figured it was time to join the party." She was holding an Ingram MAC-10 in her right hand, and from the way she was handling it, the soldier knew she'd used it before.

Bolan stared at her and whispered, "What are you doing here?"

"A Mr. Brognola called for the third time and told me to go and find out if you were still alive," she said in a casual tone.

"Do you always take orders from people you don't know?"

"I do when they concern a Mike Belasko, for whom there's a 'hands off' directive from Langley," Lawrence replied.

"Mr. Brognola gave me a quick rundown on the nuclear scientists. I made some calls. A helicopter service that usually does work for the petroleum companies airlifted four men to a small farm in the Talysh Mountains, south of Baku."

The Executioner checked his wristwatch.

"Lay flat," he warned. "Fireworks in two minutes. We can talk afterward."

The two women and Bolan pressed their bodies against the ground and waited.

The seconds ticked by until a violent explosion erupted, tearing part of the roof from the building. Bolan, Tolstoy and Lawrence could hear the repeated popping sounds of ammo and rockets exploding, and the screams of men who were victims of shrapnel.

As they watched, men ran screaming out of the building, their faces and bodies bleeding. Bolan could see that Haverford and Yaneri were scarred by the ricochet of ammo rounds exploding all around them. Their faces and hands had sustained burns, but both were still alive.

Tolstoy kept staring at the door, searching for someone.

A tall, dark-skinned man in a police major's uniform, now shredded from the series of explosions, rushed out of the building. His face was filled with terror as he ran toward where Bolan and the two women were hiding.

Tolstoy got to her feet and looked at him.

The Azeri police major stared at her in shock. "They said you were dead," he gasped.

"They were wrong, Rasul. So was what you did."

Terror filled the Azeri's face.

"I had to do it, Irina. You don't know how expensive it is to put your niece and nephew through the university," he whined.

"Is that how Tamara died? So you could get money for your children's education?"

"I never turned her in. When the KGB interrogated me about Tamara, I swore she was as loyal to the Soviet Union as you were," he said, begging for forgiveness.

The Russian woman kept staring at the major.

"Please, Irina. I didn't know that they were going to... I thought they were just going to question you. You've got to believe me," he pleaded.

"It doesn't matter if I believe you," she said coldly, raising her pistol and emptying it into the major. "I believe you didn't care what happened to her, to me or to anybody else. I hope for their sake your children never find out what you really were," she muttered bitterly.

The Russian colonel turned away before the body collapsed to the ground.

In the distance they could hear the loud sirens of police and fire fighting vehicles.

"I think we better get out of here and have a talk with Haverford about the scientists," Bolan suggested.

The two women followed him to the Jeep.

"I'll ride with you," Lawrence said. "Somebody from the embassy can pick up my car in the morning."

Bolan barely heard her. He was watching Iranian Revolutionary Guards help Yaneri and Haverford into a military vehicle, and wondered where they were taking the two.

Wherever it was, he'd be right behind them.

Ready to fight or to talk.

The choice was theirs.

24

Bolan followed the two vehicles until they reached the Iranian ambassador's house and parked. He watched as the guards rushed Yaneri and Haverford into the large building.

He drove the Jeep down one of the small streets that ran into Nizami Square and parked it at the curb. Bolan and his companions got out of the vehicle and studied the ambassador's house.

"I've heard they keep a small army of the Republican Guards inside to prevent anyone from invading the place," Lawrence warned.

Bolan looked at her. "Got any idea of how the place is set up?"

"Some from the delivery people. Upstairs there are four bedrooms. The main floor has a big reception area, a dining room and connecting kitchen, as well as a series of offices."

"What about the basement?"

"A few years ago they had a lot of electrical wire delivered and carried down to the basement. From what I've heard, they've got a first-class eavesdropping operation going on down there."

"Anything else?"

"They've got barracks for more than thirty IRGs, and a weapons depot. The whole place is set up like the headquarters for a military operation."

Bolan looked at Tolstoy. "Are you up for this?"

Her voice had a cutting edge to it. "The American is mine," she warned.

Bolan didn't disagree. Haverford was about to pay the ultimate price.

THE TWO NUCLEAR researchers huddled near each other to stay warm. The heat from the fireplace couldn't dispel the chill in the large room.

The two Russians were frightened and bewildered. Nobody had explained why they had been rushed to the farmhouse by helicopter.

Sartov turned to the man who seemed to be in charge. He remembered hearing his name. Gilal Kurbanov.

"Why did you fly us here, Mr. Kurbanov? This is a terrible place."

Sartov wasn't sure where they were exactly. A small farm in the mountains of southern Azerbaijan.

"The man is right," the short, wide man sitting at the small dining table across from Kurbanov commented. "This is not a civilized area."

Georgi Shardnadze knew a lot about uncivilized places. A former sergeant in an elite airborne Vysotniki squad, the former native of the Georgian Republic had killed in many corners of the world. As a mercenary he had worked for the Bosnians, antigovernment groups in South Yemen, white terrorists in South Africa, Colombian drug barons and many others. As long as he was paid well, he didn't care whom or how many he was asked to slay.

He looked at Haverford's aide. "When do we leave here?"

Kurbanov slammed his fist on the table, causing the two Russian scientists to jump at the noise. "You, too? We leave when the American comes here and says we can leave.

"Besides, it's not so bad in these mountains," Kurbanov replied. "Fresh air, lots of empty space and a much simpler way of life than I have today." He sighed as he became nostalgic. "I spent much of my childhood in these mountains."

"Do they have a name?"

"They are named after the people who lived here since the beginning of time. The Talysh."

The armed guard was curious. "The old man who met us . . ."

"My uncle, Safar."

Professor Sartov voiced a complaint. "You haven't told us why we are here."

"Because your friend, Donielev, is dead. And the people who killed him would like to get their hands on you," Kurbanov replied.

"Then we are truly doomed," Sartov moaned. He turned to the other nuclear specialist. "We may as well turn ourselves into the authorities and beg for mercy."

Davidov nodded his agreement.

"Nobody is going any place until the American arrives," Kurbanov said. "I promise that you are safe here."

The two researchers looked relieved, until Kurbanov continued.

"We don't turn you over to the Iranians until they've paid," he added.

"What Iranians?" Davidov looked as if he were about to faint.

"The ones the chief sold you to. By this time tomorrow you'll be working in their laboratories in Tehran."

The two scientists looked terrified.

"Polsky was right to go back. If we had only listened to him, we could be in our own beds tonight instead of here," Davidov said, fear edging every word.

Kurbanov laughed cynically. "If you had listened to that old man, you could be where he is. In a grave."

Davidov was shocked. "Who killed him?"

Kurbanov shrugged. "Who cares?"

Sartov tried to show courage. "You can tell the Iranians they will get nothing from us," he shouted with bravado.

"A few hours with one of their interrogators will change your mind," Kurbanov said, sounding confident. "You either will cooperate or you will die screaming in agony."

YANERI WALKED into the small infirmary and watched as the doctor and his nurse bandaged the American. He had changed into a combat jumpsuit.

Haverford looked up at his visitor. "Who attacked us?"

"I'm not sure, but I have a suspicion it was somebody trying to get your two scientists back," the Iranian replied.

"How many were killed?"

Yaneri's face showed his bitterness. "Too many good men have departed to be with God. The man who did this will pay. I promise you that."

"Did you get a good look at him?"

"Enough to never forget his face. He looked like the great Satan himself."

"At least he didn't get the experts or their plutonium."

"Yes," the Iranian admitted. "That was a good thing."

"And tomorrow," Haverford added, "we can make the exchange."

"No. Tonight."

"I can't get the two men back until morning."

"I can," Yaneri replied. "A helicopter has been called to carry me to them."

"But the payoff. When do I get the money?"

Yaneri smiled. "Money. That is not the payoff, as you Americans say. This is."

He lifted his right hand from his side. In it he held a .45-caliber Colt Government Model pistol.

Before Haverford could protest, the Iranian pumped three rounds into his stomach.

The American stared in shock at the cavity where his abdomen had been, then slid off the examination table to the floor, soaking the immediate area with his blood and bits of intestines.

Yaneri looked at the stunned doctor and nurse. "Sorry for the mess. I'll have someone come in and clean it up," he said as he walked out of the infirmary to wait for the helicopter he had summoned.

BOLAN RETURNED from a trip to the Jeep wearing a canvas combat belt around his waist. Three M-67 grenades hung from clips. The pouches were filled with spare magazines for his Beretta 93-R and the Uzi slung over a shoulder, and he wore a small backpack.

The soldier gathered with the two women in the shadows created by a clump of bushes. He pointed to the building. "There are two side exits. I want each of you to cover one and shoot anybody coming out. After I've made a circle of the building, I'll cover the front steps." He started to move away, then stopped to add a warning. "And stay flat on the ground until they start moving out."

Tolstoy and Lawrence nodded their understanding and headed in opposite directions to take up their positions. Bolan removed the backpack and raced in a crouch to the tilting windows that provided light for the basement area.

Forcing the windows open with a small crowbar from his bag, the soldier pressed a brick of plastic explosive against the concrete-block wall and set the timer for ten minutes. He repeated the action at each window.

Moving swiftly to the front door, he lined the wooden frame with plastic explosive and set the timer, then moved back into the bushes to wait.

Overhead he heard the familiar sounds of rotor blades and looked up to see a helicopter working its way into the field behind the Iranian ambassador's home.

He recognized the gunship as a Russian-made Mi-34. Powered by a single 320-horsepower, nine-cylinder, air-cooled M-14V-26 engine, the Hermit utilized a semiarticulated four-blade main rotor and a two-blade tail rotor. The aircraft was capable of a cruising speed of 164 miles per hour and could travel a distance of four hundred miles.

The Hermit could carry four passengers, including the pilot. Watching the gunship slowly descend, Bolan noted the pair of light machine guns mounted on either side.

When it touched ground, a rear door of the building opened and a single man ran swiftly to the helicopter. Before the warrior could level his Uzi, the passenger had jumped into the chopper and signaled the pilot to go.

The Executioner rushed to the back of the building and emptied an entire clip at the swiftly rising gunship. He could hear the lead crash against the outer skin of the chopper, but the speed with which the rotored aircraft ascended made it impossible to bring it down with 9 mm rounds.

He had recognized the man scrambling aboard. It was Massoud Yaneri, the man he had come to bring down.

A series of explosions in the front of the house snapped Bolan back into action.

He raced around the building and watched from the safety of cover as the exploding plastique charges destroyed the sophisticated communications installation. The front door opened, and Iranian Revolution Guards ran out of the building, firing their weapons wildly.

Snapping in a fresh magazine, Bolan measured each controlled burst carefully and took out each gunner as he came into range. He heard gunfire from the other side of the building, and the anguished screams of dying men.

Bolan waited several minutes to make sure no one was left to rush out and try to become a martyr, then moved around to the right side of the building.

Seppi Lawrence was kneeling, her finger pressed against the trigger of her Smith & Wesson. She glanced up and saw the Executioner. "I don't think anybody is left to come out," she said in a flat voice.

Leading the way, Bolan went in search of Irina Tolstoy. A half-dozen uniformed bodies strewed on the ground bore silent witness to the effectiveness of the woman's accuracy.

The soldier looked for Tolstoy, then found her. He knelt beside the still form that had once been a vibrant, beautiful woman looking forward to living in a happier Russia.

A stray shot had ended her dreams on a side lawn in Baku.

He would mourn Irina Tolstoy's death later. Right now he had to find out where Yaneri was going and where the nuclear scientists were being held.

A moment later, he turned to Lawrence, but she had disappeared. Then he saw her coming out of the open front doorway toward him.

"The American Irina was looking for is in the basement. Somebody blew his life away," she reported.

He lifted Tolstoy's body to carry it to the Jeep.

"Maxwell Haverford is dead," Lawrence said as she caught up with Bolan.

He heard her, but his thoughts were elsewhere.

Setting the colonel's body on the back seat, he snapped a fresh clip into his Uzi and got into the Jeep.

The war was far from over, at least for him.

Yaneri had the scientists, but more important, Yaneri was still alive.

25

Lawrence entered the living room of her small apartment.

"I've made arrangements for Colonel Tolstoy's body to be flown back to Moscow. Mr. Brognola said he would make sure she received full credit for her services to her country."

Bolan looked up at the young woman and nodded. "She meant more to Russia than her country will ever know," he commented. "She could have stayed in the United States and built a successful career there. But she chose to return and try to help create a new Russia."

"Some people put their principles ahead of their own lives," the CIA operative commented gently.

She became curious. "Do you ever sleep? I don't think you even have a hotel room here."

"I was going to get around to that. There hasn't been time. The scientists are still missing. We need to get a line on where they've been taken."

"Let me make some calls from my bedroom while you try to grab some shut-eye. I'll wake you up when I get something useful," she promised.

Bolan watched her leave, then loosened the shoulder harness and stretched out on the couch.

He could feel fatigue slither through his body. He let his eyes close. For just a minute, he warned himself. There was too much to get done to waste time resting.

KURBANOV HEARD the rotors of a helicopter as the aircraft descended. He was pleased. It meant two things: Haverford had collected the money from the Iranians, and the two of them could return to Moscow.

Sartov and Davidov cowered in the wooden chairs. Their terror at having to spend the rest of their lives among the Iranians showed on their faces.

"Perhaps it won't be so bad," Davidov whispered to his associate. "After all, we have what they want."

The two looked at the three lead containers sitting against a wall.

Sartov leaned over to the other researcher. "Do you think they will keep us locked up in cages when we are not working?"

Kurbanov smiled. From what he knew of the fundamentalists who ran Iran, the two Russians were worrying needlessly. He suspected both of them would be executed—right after they had trained the staff of the nuclear-research laboratories.

Kurbanov heard footsteps approaching the small porch outside. He got to his feet and walked to the door. As he opened it, he expected to see Haverford, not the man standing outside, his right hand wrapped around a 9 mm mini-Uzi machine pistol.

Stunned, he asked, "Who are you?"

"The name is Yaneri. I've come for the Russian scientists and their plutonium."

Kurbanov tried to look past the stranger for his boss.

"Is Haverford with you?"

"No. He is dead. Like you." Yaneri raised the machine pistol and triggered a pair of rounds into Kurbanov's chest.

The mercenary at the table reached down and grabbed the Skorpion SMG at his feet. The Iranian Intelligence official spun to face him and emptied the rest of the magazine vertically until the merc's body was shattered by the continuous impact of high-velocity lead.

Ignoring the shower of blood and bits of bones and tissues that spattered the room, Yaneri snapped in a new clip and turned to the terrified Russian scientists.

"It's time to leave," he said coldly.

Too frightened to protest, the men got to their feet and started walking toward him.

The Iranian shook his head.

"You forgot something." He pointed to the three plutonium containers.

The scientists reached down and lifted the carriers.

Davidov managed to force a question out of his mouth. "Where are you taking us?"

"To a place where you can continue your work undisturbed."

"And when we are done?"

The Iranian smiled. "You will be well taken care of. I promise you that," he commented as he gestured for them to walk outside.

Yaneri reflected on his last words.

Well taken care of.

In a world filled with hate and turmoil, what could be better than leaving it?

He had not lied.

THE STONE BUILDING on the outskirts of Rasht was heavily guarded. Only twenty miles from the center of the small Iranian city, the structure housed a sophisticated nuclear-weapons-research center. A tall, electrified chain-link fence surrounded the one-story building. Machine guns were set in concrete emplacements on all four sides, and trained fighters manned them day and night.

Atop the structure was a bank of missile launchers, remote controlled from a smaller building that functioned as a control center, arms depot and living quarters for the three dozen Iranian Revolutionary Guards on duty.

Nuclear development was carried out on the main level, as well as in underground laboratories. A testing site was a jet-hour away from the research center in a remote corner of the Elburz Mountains.

Transportation to and from the nuclear-research center was provided by a fleet of military vehicles, as well as helicopters and small jets that arrived and departed from the small airport built a hundred yards from the chain-link fence.

Six Iranian Revolutionary Guards surrounded the building, toting Heckler & Koch MP-5 submachine guns. At least another dozen, armed with similar weapons, lounged along the roadside that passed by the guarded structure, smoking cigarettes and chatting about the women they had met on leave in the nearby city.

The unusually chilly evening had descended on them like a heavy cloud. Their thin cotton uniforms did little to help them stay warm. The men rubbed their arms and shoulders to stave off the cold.

Inside the building was a series of laboratories and living quarters. A small, plainly furnished suite was available for special visitors. The apartment had been assigned to the pair of Russian nuclear experts. Yaneri had escorted the men to their new home.

Seated on a long, uncomfortable couch, the two elderly men focused on the wall across the room, trying not to make contact with the Iranian's eyes.

The man's face filled with anger. "We have your plutonium," he snapped. "Why do we need you two?"

Dr. Davidov raised his eyes and looked at the interrogator nervously. "You don't," he said nervously. "You can send us back to face our punishment with our government."

Yaneri drew his right hand back and slapped the terrified scientist's face. "You have not experienced punishment until you meet the interrogation staff at the Intelligence Ministry,'' he warned.

He waited for the words to sink in, then smiled. ''You can both save yourselves a lot of unnecessary pain. Show our scientists how to produce this new plutonium.

''We know how to form the plutonium into a sphere—you call it a 'pit,' I believe. All you have to do is supervise the assembly of the explosives around the pit and the connecting of the capacitor devices. Then,'' he promised, ''you can leave Iran and return to Moscow, or any other country, with enough money to live out your days in comfort.''

The two scientists exchanged glances. Both of them sensed that they would live until the bomb was assembled and not a moment longer.

''Your answer,'' Yaneri demanded. ''Yes or no? If it is yes, we have a lovely apartment ready for you near the city of Qum when your work here is completed. If it is no, you will end your days in a grave beside this building.''

What Yaneri hadn't bothered telling the two Russians was that he had already decided their fate.

Death by execution.

The deputy minister waited while the two Russians whispered to each other. He had plenty of time. They did not.

MOVING IN THE SHADOWS, Mack Bolan worked his way past the lounging troops. In blacksuit and combat cosmetics, he was almost impossible to spot at night.

Seppi Lawrence's contacts in the *mujahedin* underground movement had pinpointed this location. The helicopter she had lined up had brought him to a makeshift landing site in Rasht.

She had wanted to accompany him.

''No.'' His reply was firm, with no room for arguing. ''You do represent the United States government.''

''I could leave a letter of resignation,'' she suggested.

''You're more valuable doing what you've been doing.''

"But what if you don't come back?"

"Tell Hal Brognola what happened."

The *mujahedin* had agreed to drive the Executioner to the secret nuclear-research lab.

"We can provide you with armed men to assist you," Abdul Akmal, the local *mujahedin* commander, had offered.

"I'd do better alone," Bolan replied, rejecting the offer.

"Whether or not you want us, we plan to be there. Not for you but for our country and for the sane people of the world," Akmal replied.

The soldier sensed that even endless hours of arguing wouldn't change the underground leader's mind.

"Just keep out of my way."

As the three vehicles, all filled with armed *mujahedin* fighters, turned off the main highway and onto the poorly paved road that led to the secret facility, Bolan had the feeling that his mission was about to come to an end.

The only thing he didn't know was if he would still be alive when it was over.

His targets were inside the building, according to the *mujahedin*. One of their members worked as a cleaning woman at the research site. She had been ordered to get a small suite ready for two important visitors, and another suite ready for a top government official.

For Bolan, that meant that besides the two scientists, a bonus was waiting for him this night: Massoud Yaneri, deputy minister of the Iranian Intelligence Service, and his personal squad of fanatical Iranian Revolutionary Guards.

One of them, a sour-faced, middle-aged man, was leaning against a small road marker.

Moving quietly behind him, the Executioner dispatched him with a swift slash of the Applegate-Fairbairn blade across his throat. Easing the uniformed body to the ground, Bolan surveyed the area.

Akmal moved to his side. "What do you want us to do?"

Bolan didn't answer him immediately.

There were too many guards in sight—and inside the building—to kill in direct battle. Even with the dozen *mujahedin* who had insisted on coming with him.

He came up with another plan. "When your men hear the explosives go off, have them kill every IRG they can. It has to be quick, before anyone can call for backup."

"We will also destroy the communications dishes on the roof," Akmal said, and vanished into the shadows.

Moving swiftly to the rear of the building, the Executioner worked a small block of C-4 plastique around the door-handle mounting, until it looked like a flattened wad of clay. Inserting a miniaturized detonator and timer, he set the tiny clock for five minutes, then moved back to the front.

Easing a pair of HE M-67 grenades from his combat harness, he pulled their pins and counted to five, then tossed the bombs in a high pass to the opposite end of the building and flattened himself against the stone wall.

The exploding fragments shredded five nearby IRGs and shot heated darts of shrapnel into four more. Their screams shattered the night, and a sense of confusion and panic erupted.

Guards posted along the roadside rushed back into the compound, firing their weapons at any sign of movement. Four more guards fell to the wildly fired volleys of their own comrades.

Concentrated fire drilled into the confused IRGs. Even without nightscopes, the *mujahedin* fighters were reducing the size of the opposition.

Explosions on the roof of the building meant that the underground fighters had managed to destroy the communications system of the complex.

Two of the IRG soldiers dashed to machine-gun emplacements and opened fire on the darkness beyond the compound. The sounds of screams was proof that they were striking back at the attacking force.

Bolan crouched and moved swiftly to the nearest machine-gun site manned by the IRG. Pulling the pin on a grenade, he tossed the bomb overhand like a softball. Exploding as it made contact, the missile dismembered the body of the man who had sat behind the 7.62 mm RPK light machine gun.

The soldier started to move toward the other manned emplacement, then saw a pair of underground fighters overwhelm the gunner. One of them had a bayonet in his grip, and kept plunging it in and out of his adversary's body.

Clustering into a circle, the remaining IRGs waved their automatic rifles in the air and searched for the enemy. A side door opened, and another dozen armed guards poured into the night, pumped up for combat.

The Executioner didn't make them wait. A fourth high-explosive grenade fell into their midst. Before they could escape, the bomb exploded, killing another four of the ragtag soldiers.

"An army is attacking," a junior officer shouted in Farsi. "Take cover."

Wave after wave of lead rained on the defenders from beyond the electrified fence. One by one the confused soldiers fell to the ground.

The battle was becoming a rout. The remaining IRGs rushed to escape through the chain-link fence. Their bodies crackled with electricity as they made contact with the high voltage flowing through the fence.

One of the men ran back into the building and shut off the line that fed electricity to the fence. Bodies that had been glued to the metal of the barrier were now free to fall back to the ground.

The handful who still lived tore open the gate and ran into the night. Bolan accelerated their race from the area with a spray of well-placed zingers from his Uzi SMG. Four more guards fell. No one stopped to help them to their feet or check if they were dead.

From the darkness the soldier could hear the sounds of fire, the screams of dying men as the *mujahedin* fighters vented their vengeance on their former enslavers.

The front door opened. A frightened man in an Iranian major's uniform poked his head out.

The Executioner exploded it like a pumpkin with a trio of parabellum rounds that cored into the man's skull. With an eerie screech from almost-dead lips, the shattered head fell inward.

Bolan made his move. Ramming a fresh magazine into the Uzi, he rushed the front door, kicking it open with a booted foot and spraying the area inside with hot lead.

A uniformed guard crouching beside a wooden chest against a wall danced a macabre jig of death, then fell to the floor, his chest ruined.

Bolan could hear several shots from behind the thick wooden door next to where the guard had been standing. Rushing to it, he rammed a muscled shoulder against the door and shoved it open.

Another door at the opposite end of the room was open. Bolan scanned the room and saw the two bodies, recognizing the dead pair from official photographs: the two missing scientists who had tried to stage their own kidnapping.

They'd paid the ultimate price.

He quickly looked for the plutonium containers. They were gone.

The soldier started for the open door, then checked his wristwatch and stopped. Kicking the door shut, he dropped to the ground and waited.

The explosion blew the thick rear door from its hinges. Shattered remnants of a body flew through the opened doorway.

Outside, Bolan could hear the screams of whoever had been hiding there. Walking gingerly among the shredded body parts, he found what he'd been looking for.

Three badly dented lead containers and what was left of what looked like had once been Massoud Yaneri.

It was a bitter victory.

A woman he'd grown to admire had made the ultimate sacrifice. But three deadly men the world couldn't afford to let live were also dead.

It was unfortunate that the nuclear scientists had perished, but on the other hand, the knowledge they possessed was as dead as they were. It didn't bother the Executioner at all that it would take the Russians many years before they could duplicate their results.

He examined the lead containers. They looked solid. The helicopter flight from Rasht to Baku traversed the Caspian Sea. Not a bad potential burial site.

He'd have to make a decision about what to do with the containers before he caught up with Hal Brognola.

It was time to leave.

There was no way that he could solve the problem of the mafia in Russia, any more than he could eliminate organized crime in his own country.

But he had made a small dent in the formerly impenetrable armor of the Russian mafia gangs. It was up to the Russians themselves to continue to fight back.

He did not hold out much hope for the future. But maybe he would be proved wrong. Only time would tell.

Exiles from the future in the
aftermath of the apocalypse

JAMES AXLER

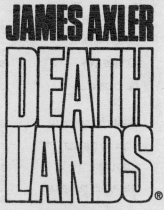

Stoneface

In 2001, the face of the earth changed forever in a nuclear
firestorm. Generations after the apocalypse, Ryan Cawdor leads
the courageous struggle for survival in a brutal world, striving to
make a difference in the battle raging between good and evil.

In the Deathlands, the war is over...but the fight has just begun.